East of the City of London and Beyond: WWII Through the Eyes of a Child

Eddie Chambers

New Generation Publishing

FOREWORD

"Once upon a time…" that's how many children's stories begin, the fictional ones, that is and so does my story. Mine however is not a storybook though but the real one, the one of my life or part of it. I cannot think of any better way to convey the impression, in my misty memory, of when and what was my earliest childhood recollection. So again, once upon a time…. there was a little baby boy called David, barely two weeks old, who was very, very poorly and Mummy told me that he was going away to be with Jesus. I was sad about that and so was she and I can just remember it and the fact that David was my younger brother. There you have it, my first conscious memory and because of the event I can date it, too. It was 2nd October 1938, I was only 3 years and 7 months old. David did go to be with Jesus but that it was the second younger brother to leave us in the same way, albeit at a slightly older age, was not in my awareness or understanding of that time. I shall expand on that later as the 'living ever after' part, happy or otherwise, of my story unfolds

The decision to record what follows in this book was not a single conscious thought but rather one that grew upon me from a series of thoughts and over a period of time. Not the least of my reluctance to do so, was the firm conviction that it would be of no interest or consequence to anyone else to be able to read of my life's events, happenings, history or otherwise. However, the 'growing upon me' process was motivated firstly by a desire to provide my children, my grandchildren and so on with the material to establish family history and so forth, should that become their desire. My own identical quest was hampered by the absence of any such record and my own neglect to 'plunder' parents and relatives' memories before they passed on.

The second motivation was the unexpected interest of my family members and friends and the third motivation, was the specific interest of so many of them in the period involved that included the Second World War. The reluctance was set aside therefore, and the task of writing was undertaken to the best of my ability. I have no book writing skills or pretences to becoming an author to carry me through but just the plain and simple process of recording memories, describing various events, happenings, scenarios, impressions, people, the times and the faces of and in, the first 18 years of my life. The main title, attributed to this collection of my memories of my childhood, is meant to convey to the reader several things. Firstly, that the writer was born, bred, educated and for many years lived, in the locality of the part of East London closest to the City of London itself, the so-called "square mile". The City's eastern boundary, in fact, starts at Aldgate Pump, once situated just outside one of the original gates of that name of the walled city of yesteryear. A more personal significance of Aldgate Pump, because of later relevance, is expanded upon much further in my narrative, which the reader will not miss. Secondly, to state that childhood is all about people relationships and not just surroundings, places or daily circumstances and that despite some belief to the contrary, children from densely populated situations, ably overcome restrictions of space and environment to still have a memorable, meaningful childhood. Then thirdly, to establish the intense pride of the writer, in qualifying to be called an "Eastender" which is often misapplied to anyone from anywhere in the area East of London, even into the county of Essex! That said, inevitably, because of the span and the enforced changes imposed by WW2, some of the memories of my childhood, feature in places away from the East End itself, although not away from areas East of London. Nevertheless, the links with the area remain resolute and relevant, even in those episodes, because of the continuous presence of family members in East London and because even if I was removed in body for a time, I was never removed in spirit.

The format of this record is in 3 separate parts, each with its own title page. The trip down memory lane begins, with my very first recall of events as a child, just prior to the war, carries on into and through that epic period and then closes post war, the family re-united and as the writer enters the teenage years. The third phase sees those teenage years described until the writer is claimed for National Service in the Royal Air Force. So, read on and hopefully, enjoy, at least as much as I did in writing it all down. If not, then I'm sorry!

Eddie Chambers
Folkestone, Kent. March 2017

Enjoy the read!

Best wishes,

Eddie Chambers

THE PREDECESSOR OF ALDGATE PUMP?

This is the Standard, as it was called, which probably predated the present Aldgate Pump and was sited further west at the junction of Cornhill, Bishopsgate and Gracechurch and Leadenhall Streets. Erected in 1582, it had a water cistern with 4 spouts and was supplied by lead piping from the nearby River Thames - for drinking also you may well ask? Road mileage measurements for all routes eastwards out of London were taken from this point.

This is an actual photo and shows Aldgate Pump in 1880, situated at the fork in the road, of Aldgate, Leadenhall Street and Fenchurch Street, at or very close to the spot of the present standing of the Pump and the one of my memory.

Having just used an iconic picture of a London feature, that just happens to have a significance to me and my record of memories, I cannot resist inserting another. This one has specific relevance to all indigenous 'Londoners' of the time, and in fact has become associated worldwide with London. I refer to the red London bus of course! Having lived in London for so many years of my life, I have witnessed many varieties of passenger transport, from the bus of the late 1930's to the tram, then the trolleybus and through to present day variants. This is the main reason I always looked forward to going to or near the Aldgate Bus Garage. However, I thought I would just insert a picture of the very first bus type that I can ever remember, notably because of the uncovered staircase at the back. I just loved climbing that staircase, as slowly as I could in anticipation of the exciting view. There are several in the above picture that closely match what I was used to, however those had the upper deck covered, with just the staircase being left open.

My Roots, and those first childhood recollections...

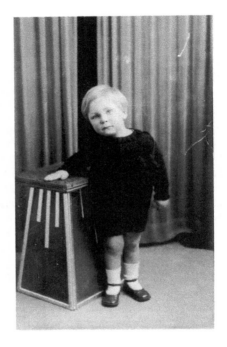

I am not famous, infamous, especially talented or even nondescript. Most people like me, I get on well with virtually everyone that I meet or come to know, am well loved by my wife and family and I adore every one of them in return. Like everyone, I have attributes and failings, but most are inconsequential in the context of this book. I was well educated, have been quite notably successful in business, have stayed active and healthy for much of my life and am fully retired. In short, I am just an ordinary bloke, really, with some ordinary recounting of life to reveal but prompted, shall we say, to tell the tale by several to begin with and then urged on by others later. With such a mundane introductory paragraph, the earliest response from any reader that this literary work will evoke verbally or otherwise, will probably be something like my own quizzical exclamation spoken out loud, "So, whose silly idea was this in the first place?" Whatever will be the reader's next reaction, I dare not contemplate and for my response to myself to this question, at the time of posing it – read on. The opening thrust of this manuscript is all to do with establishing or justifying, if you like, just why I should put pen to paper or more correctly, fingers to keys on the subject of 'my life story?' Unashamed ego perhaps, maybe an astounding tale to tell, a very tentative belief that it might just gel with readers, were all possible reasons but not conclusive ones. As well, I would be using the mind and language of an adult to describe those crucial early years and memories, so would I get it right as it really was? Next, as a child I became a Christian and writing now as an adult, I would want to record what a difference that made in my life and how I firmly believe that God had His hand upon me from the very beginning, whilst not fulling grasping that fact at the time. Maybe most significant of all, was not so much establishing a reason for doing it but how to go about it and even begin the process, anyway? What approach to make, what style to adopt and where to start, being the three prominent issues in my mind? After not too much agonising along these lines, I decided to do it anyway and for what, for me, was the most justifiable of causes. Having greatly regretted, in later life, my own failure to question and glean from my parents, grandparents, aunts and uncles, older relatives and family friends, all that I could about their lives and backgrounds, whilst they were still around, prompted me to put it all down in writing for my children, all my grandchildren and other family who would survive me and might just like to know – even if it did not occur to them just now, as had been the case with me. The bonus from making this decision was, that I needed not to worry about whether my story was interesting, astounding, attention grabbing or just down-right, boringly ordinary. My family would be forgiving enough to at least read what I would write, wouldn't they? So, the first conclusion reached, the other two issues that needed sorting just fell into place. First, my approach to the task would be to record memories, flash backs so to speak, from as far back as I could recall and as chronologically accurate as I could make them. I could embellish the narrative with my feelings, impressions and attitude at the various times plus describe or refer to coincident major events both historical or personal. This would help to provide an overall atmosphere and context to the mental picture of the readers – my family members or anyone else, for that matter! Secondly, as for where to start, well that took a little longer to decide upon but I resolved that that should be from my earliest actual recollection, my first identifiable memory. However, I would tackle the whole project from when I became eighteen years of age and work back from there, treating this as being a good concluding point; the end of my childhood, my further upbringing and the teenage years of my life thus leading into my going into the RAF for National Service. This would be the precursor to the 'becoming of age' period of my life, twenty-one years old in those days and starting my adult life for real, with all that that would entail and a totally different story. Surely, a very good point at which to stop the clock, too, look back and let the memory banks begin to unroll, slowly come into focus, pinpoint that first definable memory and for my fingers to begin to translate the pictures into words.

One of the Brylcreem Boys

It was 6th. April 1953 and I stood on the platform of London's Euston station alongside my girlfriend, Eileen, with a mixture of emotions tumbling through me, among them being uncertainty, misgivings, sadness and not a little nervousness, as well. After all I was leaving home and my family, again. I say again because I had done this before and I don't mean just for a few days or a holiday. I mean to live and stay somewhere else away from my home, my family and friends for an extended period, just like I had done 13 years before during the Second World War. I had been evacuated to Swindon and then gone to live with my Aunt and Uncle, in Upminster, to see out the war, leaving most of my near family in London and with my father eventually many more miles away, in the Army overseas. How all that came about and much more, will be explained as you read on. This time, now much older but still only a young man of 18, I was going away at the command of the government to serve two years of National Service in the Royal Air Force. In the parlance of the time, I was to become one of the 'Brylcreem Boys', the slogan attached to all members of the RAF, as in the advertisement of a smart uniformed airman and as per Denis Compton, England Cricketer, with immaculate styled hair held in place by 'Brylcreem' hair dressing!

I cannot be too precise about my thoughts and feelings at the time of my first long stay away, back in those wartime days but as I was going to stay then with well known and loved family, I doubt that there was the same degree or range of misgivings and apprehension in my mind, as on this occasion. What would it be really like this time? Would I be able to cope with all those restrictions of military life on my freedom, being loudly ordered and bossed about, made to do seemingly pointless things, made to go anywhere at any time and, maybe, even abroad – although that was not such a bad thought, really, was it? What would the food be like? How about looking after the daily things of life, like washing and ironing my clothes, mending and darning socks and such like? But this was no real threat – Mum had taught me well! However, how would I take to a whole new regime, much harsher and unforgiving than what I had been used to? Would I get 'homesick' and or 'girlfriend' sick? What sort of treatment was I going to get when others learned that I was an active Christian and went to church? Some of these things we talked about, standing on the platform, as well as when I would be likely to come home on leave plus just idle chatter, as the time to board the train got nearer. Then it was time to say goodbye: a kiss, a long hug and the feel of something being pushed into my hand with words something like, "You won't get much pay, and this will help a bit".

I got onto the train that was going to take me to Wolverhampton, where I would change for another that would land me up at Hednesford, in Staffordshire. This was the RAF station at which I would have to discard my civilian clothes and step into the uniform of an Aircraftsman Second Class (AC2) and endure, with many other poor souls, my basic training or in popular parlance, 'square-bashing'. Mind you, I could say that I was already favoured because, at least, I was going into the service of my choice, not always the case in the experience of many of my contemporaries. I was given to understand that a grammar school education and 'O' levels were the reasons for that and caused me to also be drafted into what was called 'POM' Flight – yes, we called it that, too! It grandly stood for Potential Officer Material – oh, well! I waved out of the window of the carriage for as long as I could see Eileen and then I sank onto the seat and I can only guess, now, what was going through my head as the clackety-clack of the wheels on the rails began the inevitable background sound to the apprehensive monotony of the journey. It was the 6th. April 1953, as I said, I was just eighteen years, one month and 7 days old and on my way to begin another significant chapter in my life. Oh, and by the way, that pay that Eileen had referred to on the platform, when she pressed some money into my hand? It was to be one pound, eight shillings per week or one pound forty pence in today's money – four shillings or just twenty pence a day!

I was a man by some reckoning, although at that time 21 was still recognized as being the real coming of age event. So, what had happened in the preceding years, to bring me to this significant landmark in my life? When, where and how had it all begun, at least as far as my memory could take me back? The Second World War had ceased almost eight years ago but where had I been since, during and before that? What had I done in my eighteen years, one month and six days? What events had shaped, moulded and influenced me into the person that I was, as I arrived at RAF Hednesford to serve

Queen and Country in her Majesty's Royal Air Force? What had happened to my family, as well, during my initial, early, informative and adolescent years? To begin to answer those questions I must record that it all started like this.

HOW IT ALL BEGAN – GRANDPARENTS AND PARENTS

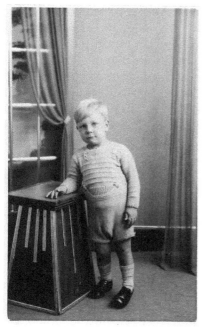

Researching family history is now not only a desirable exercise as never before, not only a hobby or even a project to embark upon in interest or curiosity. It is a money-making business if you are on that side of it and jolly expensive and time consuming, if you are on the searching, discovering side. Yet, I have only begun to research, with my remaining family members, the in-depth origins and background of my grandparents, that is George and Bessie Ayres on my mother's side nor those on my father's side, another George and Florence Chambers. My paternal grandfather, my grandmother's second husband, died when my Dad was quite young and so I never knew him and my grandmother, Florence. I never got close to either, unusually so for most grandparents. She was a very private sort of person, a bit gruff in manner but always kind to me and to children generally and with the war years intervening, we never actually got to see her a great deal and she also died in 1950. I suspect that this act of putting down in print, as many of my childhood memories as I can, may well arouse an interest in tackling the subject of family roots and ancestry – we'll see. Notwithstanding, I shall initially attempt to set the scene, from what I have learnt from others, of course, at least for the entrance into the world of the very first grandchild – a grandson, at that – yours truly.

My maternal grandfather Ayres, as far as I can presently ascertain, was an adopted child by a family named Gales, so how or why he had the surname of Ayres is very much a family mystery and how true remains to be ascertained. There are hints of further intrigue in that adoption father Gales, told my grandfather that he was the illegitimate son of a very wealthy man, a property owner in South West London (Clapham or Streatham area) and a maid servant and that one day the inheritance could all be his. Not unlike the many similarities, it seems, to "upstairs, downstairs" scenarios often heard of in those times. However, the "one day" failed to arrive, it so transpired, and Grandad grew up in much more ordinary surroundings but what brought him to East London and the intriguing change in name will feature very strongly on the family history trail, methinks. The area or location of his adopted roots it seems was in Wapping, where the Gales family seemingly served as Wardens of a Seaman's home or possibly even a Work House.

My grandmother's family name was Mitchell, David and Elizabeth were her parents and they hailed from Ilford, Essex I believe and several of my great aunts and uncles, all lived in that county. However, there is firm evidence that the Poplar area of East London figured strongly in my grandmother's early life, together with her two brothers and three sisters. From other known facts that I can verify, it seems that George and Bessie Ayres (as she became) probably met in or around the early nineteen hundred's and were married on 28th.September 1905, both being 23 years old according to the marriage certificate. They lost their first child, Bessie, born in February 1907; their second, my Aunt Lily came along in August 1908, my mother, Gertrude, the third child was born in December 1909, followed by my Aunt Grace, in August

14

1916 and, finally, my Uncle Leslie in February 1922. When my grandparents met, my grandfather was working as a Porter in the Children's Hospital in Hackney Road, where my grandmother was a nurse and later became a qualified midwife. It then transpired that my grandfather became a Porter in residential flats in Bethnal Green, owned by the East End Dwelling Co. before taking on the role, now married to my grandmother, of resident Caretakers of a disparately owned block of flats, College Buildings, backing onto the well-known Toynbee Hall in Wentworth Street, Aldgate, in East London. The other end of this street is more famously named as Petticoat Lane. These flats and the buildings of this area are steeped in history, infamous at times, like 'Jack the Ripper' territory and both the flats and the area feature heavily in my childhood, as I shall relate later. I have unearthed the following two illustrations of College Buildings, one a photo and the other an artist's impression. So, let me add a little detail to those pictures. It seems that there were 87 flats, in College, on the ground and 4 upper floors in what were known as East, Centre and West Block, with each block separately owned; West Block by the adjoining Toynbee Hall, East Block by the Co-operative movement and the Centre Block by another body or organization, that I know not the name of.

I have hand-drawn two layout and contents plan which, hopefully, will enable the reader to visualise the scenes inside my grandparents flat, at around 9.15pm in the evening of the 21st. October 1940.

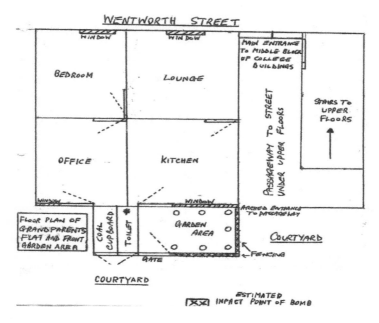

WENTWORTH STREET

BEDROOM

LOUNGE

MAIN ENTRANCE
TO MIDDLE BLOCK
OF COLLEGE
BUILDINGS

PASSAGEWAY TO STREET
UNDER UPPER FLOORS

STAIRS TO
UPPER
FLOORS

OFFICE

KITCHEN

FLOOR PLAN OF
GRANDPARENTS
FLAT AND FRONT
GARDEN AREA

COAL CUPBOARD

TOILET

WINDOW

GARDEN AREA

ARCHED ENTRANCE
TO PASSAGEWAY

COURTYARD

FENCING

GATE

COURTYARD

ESTIMATED
[XX] IMPACT POINT OF BOMB

The first plan identifies the positioning of the 4 main rooms of the flat, the small front garden area, the outside toilet and coal cupboard. Next to this is the arched entrance to the passageway that went under the upper floors of the building and into the street.

From the time that the air raid warning had sounded, just before 9 o'clock, some neighbours and friends had gathered in the lounge, together with my parents and my aunt and uncle. My baby sister, Lilian, was asleep in her pram, in the bedroom. She had been put down by my grandad after cradling her to sleep – his usual practice!

The second plan sets the scene in the kitchen where my grandad had then returned to his favourite chair in front of the range fire in the kitchen. This was to prepare to listen to Winston Churchill's wireless broadcast, through the open door to the lounge. I was asleep on a mattress bed, on the kitchen floor, just the other side of the table between my grandad and myself. A 250lb bomb, one of a stick, fell into the courtyard almost immediately outside the kitchen window of the flat. The resulting explosion caused the death of my grandfather and lesser injuries to 3 others; a lady who was in the toilet (marked as * on the plan) who lost an eye and an arm, myself with bomb splinters in my upper right arm and a neighbour, not in our flat, with chest injuries from which he also died 2 weeks later. Finally, my grandad's body was found, by rescue workers, buried under the rubble, in the doorway of the lounge door and marked on the plan with a large "X". My mother found me, in my bed, also buried under rubble and the kitchen table.

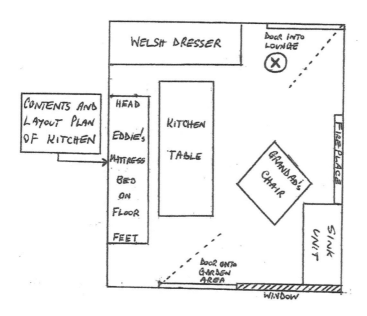

This picture of a 1950's street scene, from the front cover of a collection of East End photos, shows the frontage of College Buildings. In the foreground is 'Old Mendel' who played the old classical 78's records on his wind-up gramophone. I remember him so well.

This artist's impression is quite accurate, as my memory serves me. Just to the right of the head of the man in the center foreground, is the central archway entrance that ran through to the courtyard. This entrance had lockable iron gates that my granddad would lock each night. Immediately to the right of that, behind another man's figure, is a window. This was the front room of the flat and

COLLEGE BUILDINGS
WENTWORTH STREET

the one in which most people were seated on the night that the bombs

I believe that there were mostly 2 or 3 roomed flats with no bathroom, in fact no running water but with one big sink and a cold water tap on each landing plus communal toilets and I vaguely remember there being three or four of these. The Centre Block was the most familiar in my memories because we lived on the second floor, in No. 38 and on the third in No. 62, as well as the ground floor in No. 3 at separate stages of my early childhood. The central stairway to the upper floors, led from the ground floor in that gated archway that ran through, from the street outside and into the inner courtyard. Just next to this archway was situated the flat occupied by my grandparents, also with three rooms, mains water and a private, outside toilet opening into the courtyard (all Caretaker perks, no doubt!) Next to the toilet there was a large coal cupboard and next to that a single roomed Caretaker's Office, which was also accessed from the flat. Just at about the outbreak of WW2, two surface (as opposed to an underground) brick-built shelters were erected, in the courtyard. I have elaborated on these location details to assist in orientation, in respect of the main wartime story concerning College Buildings, later in my record. It is also very relevant, in that a fair chunk of my first childhood days were spent in these buildings, either living there or staying with my grandparents and thus was the scene of some of my earliest childhood recollections. Topically, the next photo was taken from the top balcony of College and is the scene of the street outside College Buildings in 1934/5.

This photo reveals the street scene, pre war with the little shops frequented by the Ayres and Chambers families. A tram like the one in the picture knocked my 12-year-old mother over in Commercial Street, swept her aside from going under the wheels, with the so called "cow catcher" but straight under the wheels of a motorbike. She suffered a broken collar bone. On the corner behind the tram is M.Van Oestren's cigar makers and the continuation of Wentworth Street, known as Petticoat Lane.

To return to the people in my story, I am certain that my grandfather did not serve in the armed forces, in the First World War and this was due to his being medically unfit to do so - he suffered from epilepsy. I never remember him as a very robust man either and there was talk of him having been a rather ailing person, often suffering also from severe migraines etc. My grandmother, on the other hand was a strong person, authoritative and assured and would have made a superb Matron in a hospital - who knows, she may well have so been in her time, as a qualified nurse and midwife? She ran the office side of the Caretaker's responsibilities and Grandad saw to all the practical matters, decorating, repairs and day to day maintenance and cleaning. All the Ayres children went to good schools, Leslie and Grace to Sir John Cass's, in the City of London for instance and were well educated. My Aunt Lily was also very ailing in her childhood, suffering a lot with back trouble and spending a lot of time being wheeled around stretched flat on a whicker carriage. She later improved sufficiently to work in Selfridges in Oxford Street before marrying my Uncle Bert, in 1930 and moving out to live in Upminster, in Essex but they had no children. This is significant for me for I was to spend a lot of time with them when very young, when my parents were finding life very difficult and I was to live with my Aunt and Uncle for some four or so of the war years. My Aunt Grace served in the ATS initially and then the American Red Cross all during WW2 but never married, it seems due mainly to two traumatic romance experiences, the one a tragic loss of a Guardsman boyfriend (very close) on the infamous "Death Railway" in Thailand and the other, an equally shattering encounter but for different reasons, with an American GI who turned out to be married already in the USA. My Uncle Leslie originally went into the RAF but came out on medical grounds and married my Aunt Maria in 1942 and I remember being taken to their wedding and their marriage produced two children, my cousins Carol and Beverley. Finally, this brings me to my mother.

My mother was not particularly academically gifted, but she was a real worker and the practicalities of life were her strength and forté. She was strong and robust, taking after her mother and, from what I can gather, was greatly leaned upon for help and support in the family home. She helped with the problems with my Aunt Lily's incapacity and in the bringing up of a younger brother and sister. Such a grounding stood her in good stead, no doubt, as it led her to work as a "nippie" (silver service waitress) in Lyons Corner Houses, after training in the famous Head Office, Cadby Hall and, I believe, was so employed when she and my father met. The meeting took place in Fairfield Hall, apparently, a main assembly place of the Plymouth Brethren that the Ayres family belonged to, very close to my father's home in Blondin Street, Bow and also frequented by my father, having been invited there by a friend. Mum and Dad were married in December 1933, in Whitechapel Church, just a short distance from my mother's home, in College Buildings.

This is an artist's sketch of St Mary's, Whitechapel with just a glimpse of the street corner sited, open air pulpit. The church was partially destroyed by bombing and finally demolished in the 1970's, although the perimeter wall remains to this day.

As recorded elsewhere, they produced yours truly in March 1935, followed by John, Edwin in June 1936 (John died 7 months later) then came David, Alfred in September 1938 (David died after just 2 weeks) then next was Lilian, Gertrude in June 1940 (Lilian died in 1999, just 59) and, finally Ruth, in December 1946 and still with me today– the family Chambers! At this point I will turn to my father's side of the family.

My knowledge of my paternal grandparents is much sketchier but again, the family history trail may reveal more – again, we shall see? As I have already noted, my paternal grandfather George, a dock laborer appears to have died relatively early in my father's life, leaving my grandmother, Florence, a widow to bring up two sons and a surviving daughter of twins plus, from the previous marriage to William

Kennedy, I think, three sons. So, my father Edward, George the eldest, born in December 1912, was followed by Alfred in August 1914 and then twins again in March 1920 of whom only Lillian survived. My grandmother Chambers must have had to work very hard at mundane jobs such as cleaning etc. to manage the extended family. I remember my father telling me that he and his brother often shared shoes and clothes, on alternate days to go to school in. My father did get to attend North London Polytechnic studying for the building trade but had to leave and go to work, as did his brother when the father died, to support the family. I am not sure what my Uncle Alf was employed as but he was married to my Aunt Betty in August 1938 and served in the Army in the Tank Corps and was wounded in action in North Africa, I believe. They had three daughters, Beryl, Pamela and Catherine. My other Aunt Lily, Dad's sister, did factory work, married my Uncle Charles in February 1942, who served in the RAF and had four children of whom only Linda and Kenneth survived. I believe the three half-brothers from my grandmother's Kennedy marriage named George, Ernest and Bert all served in the Navy during WW2 and one was torpedoed but survived.

My father did go on to work in the building trade and stayed in it for all his working life. However, with a lot of acquired knowledge, a good mathematical brain but sadly, no formal qualifications, it was a hard struggle for him to scale the employment ladder and the early years of my parent's marriage, both work and accommodation wise, was a real struggle. They started off in Bow where I was born, and I can then remember living in Ilford, Poplar. No doubt my mother's parents tried to assist the budding marriage (especially when children started arriving) because of the staying in three different flats, in College Buildings, during my very early childhood.

That is how it all began for me, then! I came from shall we say, a moderately poor background but with relative solidarity, on my maternal grandparents side, of sound Bible based Christianity, of good jobs and education; followed up by parents with the same beliefs, who tried their best and worked their socks off, in those notoriously difficult times between the wars Then into and through the trauma of a world war and, finally, facing the struggles of post war Britain. During that time my parents lost two sons and I two brothers, before the war; my mother lost her father my grandfather, killed by a bomb during the war, leaving a widow to cope with all the Caretaker's work of two people and my paternal grandmother, a widow already, struggled on alone through the war, with all her sons from both marriages, away on duty in the Army and the Navy. Really, you know, before my life even got into its stride, from such stock I had so much to be grateful for right to the present day and I only have further endorsements to add to that privileged state of affairs in my life experience. I owe so much to my parents who brought me into the world; to those who nurtured me and protected me, those who contributed to or were my upbringing inspiration, those who watched me grow up, those who introduced me to Jesus Christ and bible based Christianity, to God whose care and watching over me has been constant throughout my life, it is all of these that I am indebted to for who I am and what I am. My gratitude is very clear in my mind, as I look back and is unreserved. So now, a few photographs of the people I've been going on about, all of them showing the signs of much handling-the photos, I mean! Firstly, on Mum's side...

This is me, Eddie, with my grandparents Ayres in my Aunt Lily's garden, in Upminster. Just behind them is the spot where the Anderson Shelter was erected, mentioned in one of my war stories. Just to the right of the chair back you can just make out the squatting figure of our dog, Ruff! This photograph was most likely taken in the summer of 1939 and little did we know then, that my Grandad had only about a little more than a year to live!

My Mum & Dad with six-year-old me and one-year old Lilian taken in 1941, before Dad was posted overseas and probably in Swindon, where we were evacuated. (Sorry about the eyes – someone made them into holes!)

My Aunt Grace who idolized me it seems, pictured in Paris, where she was working as a Teleprinter Operator, with the American Red Cross after serving in the ATS.

Aunt Lily & Uncle Bert, childless sadly, became virtually second parents. A picture probably taken on one of our several Devon holidays, during my 4+ years stay with them. Uncle was a gardener and 'conscientious objector' (C.O.) on religious grounds, thus excusing him from military service.

My Uncle Leslie with Aunt Marie, ever the showman and the first in the family to have a car! Taken some time in the 1950's, they lived opposite us in Petticoat Lane with their two daughters, my cousins, Carol & Beverley. My Uncle started up a vegetable stall in Petticoat Lane, a retail grocery shop and warehouse and then moved into Marketing and Sales with Smedley's Foods and

Hayward's Pickles. He finally ran his own Sales and Marketing consultancy business.

Then, some photos on my father's side…

This is my grandmother Chambers standing outside her home in Blondin Street Bow. I believe she is holding her granddaughter, my Uncle Alf's Beryl. Her dress and appearance are indicative of the hard lifestyle that was her experience for all of her life, and she was not as grumpy as she appears! She lived in this house for many years including sharing with her daughter, Lily, when she married, in one room upstairs, until she died in 1950 aged 73. We used to visit her there for tea and she had a most unique way of serving you with slices of bread at tea time. She stood the loaf of bread upright, held between her knees, cutting a slice off the loaf after spreading it with whatever, probably margarine and something else and then repeating the process – no need of a bread board for her!

This is my Uncle Alf and Aunt Betty on their wedding day in 1938

This is my Aunt Lily Chambers (I had my Aunt Lily Nunn, as well) She was a lovely nature person and I have very fond memories of her. She married my Uncle Charles in February 1942.

HOW IT ALL BEGAN FOR ME – 'THE APPLE OF HER EYE!'

The heading describes how it was, as it probably always is, at the arrival of the first child, grandchild and a boy to boot, to all the ladies that is - Mum, both Grandmas and all three Aunts of the respective families! The event took place in the first Chambers' home, a second floor flat, in a three storied house, in Vernon Road, Bow and that road still exists today but not our home – the foundations probably never recovered, as you will see. Here is a picture of my Mum standing on the front steps, presumably with neighbours but whether pre or post my arrival, I know not.

My Mum, that's her at the back – complete with apron, that's Mum all right!

The title quote "the apple of her eye" says everything really, as far as the impact of it all was concerned, on the ladies. My mother dropped ten pounds and twelve ounces of bouncy, baby boy into the family pedigree and that made an impression, for a start and probably on those house foundations! From then on, or so I was reliably informed years later, my mother had little trouble in getting baby sitters, shall we say. For whoever had usurped authority over or otherwise taken prized possession of, this new arrival on a granted temporary basis (like 'walkies' in a big pram) this blonde bruiser became "the apple of her eye" My father was pretty proud, too, or so he told me years later – I think he felt that it was all mostly down to his genes (is that how you spell it?) As for my one and only grandfather well, that was the beginning of a special bond and relationship, as you will gather, later down the track. Sadly though, not to last for anywhere near enough of my young life and so it became a regret that has followed and stayed with me ever since. In fact, I have never got over losing my Grandad before I was able to know him better, as an adult and not only as a child. To me he was the epitome of what a Grandad should look like and be like; tall and distinguished, with a neat moustache (I don't know why the latter) he never sent me away as I followed him around, he let me help him with his chores, he showed me what to do and he was my mate. I've never stopped missing him and I've tried to be like him as a Grandfather myself. That's it, no more of this self-appraisal stuff, I'm getting quite embarrassed, just writing it all down. So, I'll round it off with three early photos of the blonde bruiser himself.

Left - Eddie in March 1937 just 2 years old and right, Eddie in 1939 aged 4 years plus and growing!

Taken in January 1941 in Swindon, this is Eddie almost 6 years and Lilian just 7 months old. One of several photos taken around this time when Dad went into the Army and before being posted overseas to Gibraltar.

Anyway, I feel that enough background has been laid, perhaps enough to create something of the needed atmosphere, credibility and context to the following collection of childhood memories. It's not easy, in the light of modern-day living, to put across or describe the sort of world that it was for me to be a child in and especially because of the rate and pace of change that the Second World War brought to living and lives and the acceleration of change that has developed since. Values, morals, outlooks and lifestyles must seem light years away from the present day, as thought is given to these things but they are less than half a lifetime. Just noting a few facts, to me, exemplifies what I am saying. I know that all things are relative to something but can present day society really have any concept of the reality of a weekly wage of less than £3? Living in a rented home with no fridge, washing machine, tumble dryer, dishwasher, car, TV, many instances of no radio even and as for a record player, a wind-up one even, what! How about food? Well there was a choice here –

eat it or leave it. Eat what Mum provided or go hungry and when it was gone there was no more until the next meal and every one of those was eaten around the table, as a family to boot – not on laps or anywhere else. To own half a dozen toys, you were well off and barely a change of clothes or shoes let alone the varied, multiple choice of today, on both fronts. In fact, your "best" outfit for going out was probably what you went to school in. Holidays – what were they? There might be a few days out over the local park or trips into Epping Forest, if you were lucky. Then there is the whole business of the recognition of good behaviour. For us this did bring treats, like a fish and chip supper out or a trip to see Auntie whoever – a twopenny bus ride away. As for a reward for being good, what for, you were expected to be good, anyway. Rewards were for doing the extra or for being extra good, the thing that you did, not expected of you but volunteered – that was what rewards were for. One final word on this theme is about a major plus that me and the kids of my day did have that those of today are almost bereft of and are accelerated out of just as soon as their parents, their teachers and the state can manage it and that is a childhood! We were not burdened with decisions about fashion and what to wear; about what food to eat or when to go to bed, we were not brought into every conversation or bothered with family matters that only concerned adults, in fact such things were not even raised until we were not about. We were allowed and encouraged to be kids, to play and enjoy life in a fun way, being involved as a help with jobs and errands but not introduced to the adult world of family problems, tensions, worry, pressures, decisions, sex, what to eat, trauma, opinions or fashions and such things, so early in life as they are today. Anyway, I'm not moaning or preaching or passing judgement (not much!) just let me remind you, I am simply trying to set the scene and create an atmosphere of the days and the times of my childhood and those like me, because they're so, so different to today but which are not necessarily better, either.

EARLIEST RECOLLECTIONS

Well now, have you ever thought back into your childhood days, specifically to try to recall that very first memory, any time periods, so to speak, or sequence of events? You know, like you often try to remember in later years, about any period of your life and then try to place it in the correct chronological sequence or context? For you to remember those childhood happenings may seem impossible, they might just be difficult or are you like me, you remember as if you were flipping the pages of an old photo album, seeing clear, snapshot, picture images or flashbacks but you cannot be absolutely sure of when it was except, of course, those that are specifically dated, connected with some recorded event or happening, or are corroborated by someone else who was older at the time. That is exactly how my memories come into view, sometimes as single images or at times, as groups of related pictures. Some are insignificant, childish, most likely of little interest to anyone else and then others are more dramatic, maybe associated with happy, joyous occasions but also some with traumatic, painful or emotionally sad events. As I say, I cannot always place things into a chronological order, there may be weeks, months or even more between them, the context is sometimes awry and even checking with others has not always helped. Nevertheless, they are all very real with some so vivid, in fact, possibly the more dramatic ones, that despite what I have already said about these memories, they could have happened only yesterday – and how many times do I comment so? Nowadays, I seem to have problems remembering what really happened only yesterday, let alone some 60 odd years ago. Here goes then and I have given each one of these my flashbacks or related tales, a more specific or connected sub-title. I have also illustrated, wherever possible with pictures and photos and I hope that this helps the imaginative scene painting reactions that we all have to the written word, as we read.

THE LOST ONES

This sub title is both simple and tragic, for my parents, my wider family and for me because it refers, very simply and sadly, to my two lost brothers. I was the first-born, followed by two brothers but both died young and both from double pneumonia! It is, as far as I can ascertain, my very earliest childhood memory, not so much at that time in relation to John, the first after me, because he died in 1936 when I was only some 15 months old – that sadness came later. It was more to do with David's death, because it was in September 1938 and I was around 3½ years old then and I can remember the "doctor man", as my mother called him, often coming to see David and this was Dr.Osen the family doctor then and to so be for many years to come. For the record, we were in a ground floor flat in College Buildings, No.1, next door but two to the Caretaker's Office (as explained earlier) and so Grandma and Grandad were often in and out, as well, as little David fought his fight with pneumonia – a tall order in those days for an adult, let alone a baby. I can remember, very clearly, that the news was not good most times, when the doctor called and, I believe, this was my very first conscious emotion, just hoping that David would not go away, even to be with Jesus, as my mother was trying to explain to me might happen. Brother David did go away to be with Jesus though, at just over two weeks old and I can still feel the sadness and that first emotion, even all these years later.

I have tried very hard but cannot recall any other memories that would pre-date what I have noted here about my brother David and I find it rather compelling as I search for the words to describe now, what I felt and thought about it all, at 3½ years of age! Not easy even now but very real both then and still. Remarkably, as a result of later research a newspaper article revealed an interesting fact very relevant to the death of my two brothers. Our family doctor, Dr. Osen retired in August 1992 and an article in the East London Advertiser noted that he qualified in 1934, so he was a relatively new doctor when he attended the births of me and of my two brothers. More interesting, though, is his commented recollection of his great sadness of the many deaths, particularly of children, caused around 1937/8 by an epidemic of double pneumonia in East London – the cause of death of both my brothers, so how poignant is that?

BITS AND PIECES

I have used this heading to cover a series of innocent, day-to-day stuff that comes back to me, just snatches of memories of the little things that I can remember. This is also, of course, the period from my earliest recall, at around 3 years old to, say 5 years old, in terms of the difficulty in getting the timing and location right but I would place these recollections somewhere between 1938 and 1940. For example, I can remember when we lived in Ilford for a period, just a few miles east of London, in a flat that was the ground floor of a house and that's a picture of the house today, that follows. In the early years of their marriage, my parents moved around several times and, who can say, it may have been to escape the rent man when arrears had built up? I don't really know but I do know that times were hard, and that money was always in very short supply. I remember that on this occasion, it was winter time, the snow was laying quite thick on the ground and the lady in the house next door, was sweeping her front pathway clear of the snow. Of course, I had to go and help the lady do this job, for after all, sweeping snow was fun not work. Anyway, this willing young helper was rewarded with a whole sixpenny piece (2½p) and added to the little cash that my parents could muster, Dad was able to get a bag of coal and we had a fire that evening! On another occasion in the same house, it must have been soon after Christmas, as I remember that my Uncle Jim had bought me a clockwork train set and I can recall playing with it, with my father, on the kitchen table. We had a lit candle, I remember and stood it in the centre of the table (which must have meant no money for the electric meter) and I got Dad to move the candle off the table and onto the floor, whenever I wanted the train to go around the track, pretending that it was the night time and then bring it up again for the day time. I seem to remember my father being around more than my mother, at this time and it may have been that she was working (as a 'Nippie' she worked long hours) and my father may have been in one of his periods of unemployment – they were quite frequent! Incidentally, that is the last that I remember of seeing and playing with my new train set and it most probably went the way of quite a few things of mine in those early years, as I learned later – the pawn shop! The following is that modern day (2006) picture of the house in Ilford, the one with the car outside.

Our house had an open porch then, a pathway and a gate, just like next door. No cars parked and a proper front garden in those days. It was this pathway that I helped sweep clear of the snow and the pavement in front of the gate. This road is a busy bus route today, but I doubt that it was in 1940

Another of those everyday things that I remember was when my father and my Uncle Les sat up very late one evening, to listen to a wireless commentary and it was when we had moved back to another flat in College Buildings, No.62 maybe, on the top floor? The sports commentary was of one of the big boxing fights of the day and I cannot be sure who it was that was fighting – possibly Freddie Mills, Len Harvey or Bruce Woodcock, perhaps, big fighters of the day or perhaps one of the famous Joe Louis versus Max Schmelling fights? I remember really, I think, mostly because I was not allowed to sit up with them, but I could still hear them in the other room, getting very excited. Talking sport, another regret for me, was not being able to go with Dad and my uncle, to watch Arsenal play because I was too young, but I made up for that after the war. The family were then and have been ever since, staunch supporters of the best football team on the planet – the Arsenal and those days were glory days as well, just like the present time. I believe, too, that these must have been the days of my earliest memory recall, of that lovely bonding that kids often acquire and then covet, with their sets of grandparents. The following are some of the scenarios that I fondly think back on in my memory and which illustrate my point.

In their flat in College Buildings, I remember my grandmother cleaning the kitchen range and fire oven, with brushes that had curved handles and with this black stuff that made an incredible shine, but I got to help with the polishing part only, for some reason? This range fire had very special significance, as you will see, in a later dramatic story. I can also recall Monday being washing day and it took all day, as well. Out in the courtyard, at College Buildings, was the communal Wash House, with big butler sinks, hot water boilers with a gas ring underneath, a huge "mangle" that squeezed the water out of the clothes and rows of washing lines to hang up the clothes to dry. My favourite job was trying to turn the wheel of that mangle, tough work for a little lad, I can tell you. Another job that I enjoyed helping with, was filling up the coal scuttle with all those small, shiny pieces of coal called 'nuts' from the coal cupboard. This scuttle was a black metal one and fitted into a mahogany wooden cabinet, in Gran's front room by the fireplace, and the cabinet had a big brass handle, a drop-down front and would, no doubt, fetch a tidy sum as an antique nowadays.

This picture, of unknown whereabouts to me, illustrates the range fireplace that was in the kitchen of my grandparent's flat in College Buildings. It's just like the one that I used to help to clean and in front of which my grandfather had his favourite seat.

Then I remember being banned almost, from the "holy of holies" or the Office, as it was called, only being allowed entry when accompanied by either grandparent. This was that room, accessed from my grandparent's flat, which also had a door out into the courtyard and this door, big and painted a deep chocolate brown will also feature in a later story. It ushered tenants into where the business of rents collection and the flats' management took place. This was carried out weekly on a Tuesday I seem to remember, by two very prim, starchy, spinster ladies who rejoiced under the names of Miss Brown and Miss Burbage.   The Office matched their appearance and demeanour, plain and austere, a shrine almost and kept as such by my grandmother; with its' big lockable key cupboard holding the master keys of all the flats, the large iron security safe, the smell of polish, the immaculate shiny, big leather topped desk, large blotting pad in the centre, ink wells full of red and blue ink, pens with nibs and that long, round, black ebony ruler – however did they draw straight lines with a round ruler?

My favourite times, though, were those spent with Grandad!   On the first-floor landing of Centre Block in College Buildings, next to those toilets that I have mentioned earlier, was Grandad's workshop. I used to just love being in there with him because it was full of interesting things for little boys. There were tools and nails and pieces of wood, brooms, brushes, tins of paint, ladders and loads of fascinating things to ask questions about. My grandfather had infinite patience and tolerated this inquisitive nuisance with remarkable calm but the most intriguing thing for me was distemper, no nothing to do with the ailment suffered by dogs! All along one wall of the workshop, was a long line of low cupboards, almost like a long bench seat, not with doors but with lids that hinged upwards. When the lid was lifted there were partitioned bins underneath, some half dozen or so and each had a different colour powder in it called distemper. Whenever there was a room or something to be decorated, the cheapest wall covering of that time, was plain lining paper sloshed over with distemper and my grandfather mixed his own, with the powder and water, in a bucket. Today's equivalent being vinyl emulsion, of course. My job was to help sprinkle the powder into the bucket of water whilst he stirred it to the right consistency and watching him mix the colours to get different shades was great fun.

Then there were weekly chores like the sweeping of the stairs, the landings, the entrance archway and the whole courtyard and again, there was a task attached to this regular duty just made for a small willing helper. I used to follow Grandad around with a little hand-brush, a small shovel and a bucket, to collect up the rubbish to carry to empty into the big bin in the "shoot" cupboard. What's a shoot cupboard, you ask? Well now, every landing in the block had a "shoot" which was a metal grate covered hole in the wall, into which your rubbish was deposited. You opened the grate and a hole appeared that went all the way down into the ground floor rubbish cupboard and the rubbish dropped straight into the strategically placed bins, ready for collection by the council each week. For my grandfather all of these scenarios were a real case of "me and my shadow" and who was the shadow, well, need you ask? As it happens, strangely enough, these little chore "enjoyments" may well have been the very early character forming facet of my lifelong tendency to practicality, doing things and helping out and this particular little chore with the brush and pan, just related, was also going to feature in one of my memories of war and wartime and you will read of that in the following pages. The same courtyard mentioned is also seen in a couple of the photos featured later.

These, then, are the somewhat rambling memories from the earliest ones of my childhood prior, as best I remember them, to those that specifically relate to the period of the Second World War, when I had become that little more impressionable perhaps. But, as a lead into the next section, which does focus specifically on my wartime memories, I will relate a tale, firstly because it is quite amusing and, secondly because for the life of me, I just cannot correctly place the incident, chronologically speaking. The war was on but whether only just or a little later, I cannot recall but to tell it now is as good a time as any. I know the location, it was when we lived in the second floor flat No. 38, College Buildings and I remember that my father was not around each time this happening took place and this must have been, as I learned later, because he was probably 'fire watching' on the roof of the flats with my Grandad and Uncle Les. So, to explain and this happening took place time and time again until, I suppose, my mother somehow cured the problem and it went like this. I recall, night after night, being woken from a deep sleep by Mum because the Air Raid Siren had sounded and that meant that we were to go down into the shelter. My mother was always fully occupied with getting my baby sister, Lilian, prepared, wrapped up warm and collecting together all the things that mothers do, in such or similar circumstances. Typically, with a sleepy child but big enough to dress himself, she kept badgering me to concentrate and get myself dressed to go into the shelter, although why we didn't just put a top coat on, over our night clothes, I don't know? Perhaps the reason was that it was not a private shelter - attitudes and ways were different in those days!

To fully understand this episode you must remember that, in my childhood days, boys did not wear just 'T' shirt and jeans or other equally casual type clothing, on an everyday basis – that was for holiday time and only if it could be afforded, anyway. I wore what was virtually a scaled down version of what my Dad wore and that for school and for play, as well. So, day-to-day I wore vest and underpants, lace up shoes, knee length socks, short trousers held up with braces, a shirt with a tie and a waistcoat plus a jacket - in essence, a 3-piece suit with short instead of long trousers and you will see me dressed such, in one of the photos featured elsewhere. The first time this thing happened, so my mother told me, she had left me to get dressed as instructed. She had turned her attention back to me, after getting my sister ready only to find me fully dressed except that in the sleepy stupor of being woken up, I had somehow managed to put my waistcoat on, as my trousers! I had painstakingly done up all the buttons, as flies, after putting one leg into each armhole and was trying to work out what to do with the trousers! Just what that must have looked like, one can only guess. Night after night she had to stop me from repeating the same sleepy ritual. Even today, I can recall her saying loudly to me "Eddie, that's your waistcoat, not your trousers" as I fumbled through making the same mistake and I remember so very clearly doing it, to this day.

THAT WAS THE START...

These then, my earliest childhood recollections will provide, hopefully, a degree of insight into the sort of world that I entered and, possibly, how this most likely impacted upon me in my upbringing. Certainly, as I see it by being the first child, relevant to my parent's finances and resource levels that deteriorated badly, after the first flush of their marriage, I was still privileged with the better part of their early family life. I have little doubt that the deterioration, in terms of a non-settled home and the far more difficult employment conditions, resulting in poor, little or even no income at times, were anything but conducive to the arrival of each of my brothers or to my own further upbringing. On this particular point, I can remember my mother's sister Auntie Lily with Uncle Bert, featuring often in my life with longish stay visits to their home in Upminster, to relieve the pressure on my parents it seems, and this was just the foretaste of things to come, for me, as you will see. Whether or not the fate of each of my brothers was, in some way, influenced by the prevailing times and circumstances into which they arrived in this world, I cannot say definitively but it could not have helped. I was to get a revealing insight as I have related elsewhere. I can, as I have written already, clearly recall deep regret about David's death and as I was to learn and realise later of John's earlier death I was, therefore, doubly affected. What sort of trio would we have been, with no more than three or so years between us? As with so many regrets that we encounter in life, it is the conjecture about what might or could have been, the "if only" factor, that frustrates most of all? Therein lies my real and lasting sadness– I can dream and imagine and have done so many a time, but I just don't know. Most of the musings are very, very bold, imaginative, always positive ones and always as a threesome, though!

...NOW LET'S GO ON!

The next few years, for many people, were going to be a mixture of the most traumatic, bleak, disastrous, frightening, adventurous, impactful times and involve the most life-changing sets of circumstances that would normally take a whole lifetime to experience. The world was to be sadly launched into a war, barely 21 years after it had come out of the one that had been labelled "the war to end all wars!" and I was one of the many, many children whose lives, outlooks, attitudes and character would be influenced and formed against such a grim backdrop. In some ways, as I have remarked in the ensuing narratives, the fact of being so young at the beginning of wartime, probably spared me some of the fears and misgivings felt by grown-ups. I believe, too, that we all have the ability to diminish or even erase from the mind, the things that we find unpleasant or scary - especially children. There was one thing that was for sure, though. So many, many things, situations, places and people would change, never be the same again or would disappear altogether. This has been said and is true of course, about all periods of history and experience but this time the changes were going to be desperately, devastatingly and disastrously different. So many people would live shortened lives, experience demoralised lives and compacted lives – enduring things at a rate and on a scale never contemplated or thought possible either before or since. To bring this discourse to a close, just consider one aspect alone. Never had the ordinary civilian population en-masse, of warring countries come so close to or been so much a part, first brutal hand, of the deep horrors of global war as they were to become and be in this next six years! The First World War had seen civilians introduced to the horrors of bombing of sorts, with the Gotha bomber and Zeppelin raids but here was the beginning and a worsening procession of events of civilians at war, as had never been seen before. Remember, I'm speaking of mass occupation of many countries; 'Blitzkrieg', carpet bombing of cities, concentration camps, ghastly cruelty to POW's, the Holocaust, Hitler's 'V' weapons, to name but a few things and then, to crown it all, the atom bomb! These were all the strategies and tactics and the deadly practices of war that suddenly embraced ordinary people, miles from any so called, 'front line' or actual theatre of combat. In WW2 carnage came right into the home and to civilians, men, women and children alike in awful and shameful measure and not just to the combatants of war, the soldiers, sailors and airmen of the armed forces. Sadly, lamentably and quite literally unbelievably neither society, the nations, the world or even mankind, have learnt a lesson from it all and the dire outcomes of that fact are a common and a real, daily fear in the times in which we now live. Rather dramatically put, some readers might feel and claim? No, not really – realistic possibly, describes it better? Nowadays, to worsen it all, the horrors and scenes of war, even if enacted thousands of miles away on the other side of the world, are brought right into our homes and within hours or even minutes of the happening itself – by satellite transmission of live pictures in the digital technology age. We're no longer able to be onlookers only and untouched or divorced from events, perhaps only reading about it sometime after the happening. Historians will record it and perhaps, with some even more developed technology and format in the future, our later generations will learn of wars and tragedy and absorb it even quicker by using whatever medium any new system employs – perhaps?

From September 3rd. 1939 for me, however, this dramatic war was to be viewed, experienced and taken in through the eyes of a child, this child. I mean that it was going to impress upon and become close to me; very close, touching close, hurting close, frightening close, impossible to ignore close, deep down inside close, lasting in the memory close and very life changing close, just as it was going to be for many others and with greatly differing and influential consequences of the coming of and being that close, too! What I have written thus far brings me to the outbreak of war, in my experience and the last couple of paragraphs paint a very broad-brush overview of what war was going to be and mean – written in hindsight, of course. The grownups of that September day and certainly the young had no idea, really, of what lay ahead. I believe that there was initially a feeling, at least a hope, that it would all be over pretty quickly but there was also a foreboding that grew and grew as the situation on the Continent developed and countries and defending armies were crushed, swept aside or taken captive by the Hitler machine. Soon, the British army and thousands of Belgian, French forces and others, too, would be thrown out of Europe into Britain and this country would stand alone against the Nazi menace, for all too long before help and support arrived. Where would it all end up? Fuelled by the reports that accompanied the capitulation of mainland Europe and coupled with the fear and dread so easily engendered, this was a question in everybody's mind, from the King and Queen, down through the Government and the armed forces, to the most ordinary of men, women and children. What a blessing that what the immediate future had in store for us all, such as the Battle of Britain and the 'Blitz', let alone the long ensuing years of war, was not in the ability of mankind to foresee. What an even more significant blessing was the fact that the Britain of that day, was a far greater God fearing one than the Britain of today. For instance, the King called all the people for a National Day of Prayer at the time of and for the Dunkirk operation and on 6 other momentous occasions, when we were in dire peril. The nation responded then as they did on all the other later occasions, too. Army generals and government ministers also demonstrated such belief and faith, at other significant times and later attributed the successful outcomes to nothing less than 'Divine Intervention!'

None of this, of course, forms part of my remembered understanding at the time but history tells me that it was a significant backdrop to the beginnings of my life and, as my awareness, my education and my experience developed, so did the impact and consequence become more real and understood. Perhaps some of that impact and consequence will become evident to the reader, as my recollections have left the recesses of my mind and transformed themselves into written words on paper? The next chapters will describe events and incidents that punctuated my childhood with indelible memories and I was only one of many with similar or varied experiences and, therefore, with many similar and varied stories to tell.

WORLD WAR TWO:

"Through the eyes of a child"

As I have already explained, in the record of the earliest of my recollections that come to me, the flashbacks are mostly impossible to accurately date and this continues to be the case, as those recollections begin to relate to the period of the beginning of World War Two. This situation tended to improve, of course, for as time went on and I got older, I was more likely to register the date. Thus, chronologically assembling the scenes in my memory since, has been easier with an increased likelihood of being closer to the correct timing and sequence of the events and happenings remembered that could not otherwise be corroborated. I have tried to comment in the relevant places, as I relate my stories, when and where somebody such as a friend or relative, was able to confirm any detail that was not obvious in my memory. Inevitably, over the years since events and episodes took place, a lot of family discussion and the recall of individuals, has helped me to fill in some gaps in my own memory banks, as well. As an example, the very fact of us being at war, in 1939, was not a conscious one to me at the time, neither can I remember it being declared – I was too young for that degree of awareness even, of what war was. However, I can just remember a sense of tension and what would probably have been foreboding, in my parent's talk of things like shelters, air-raid warnings, gas masks, a nasty person called Hitler and my father possibly soon having to go away into the forces. Then later, discussions confirmed all of this and more. By the time that things began to happen in earnest, some months after the actual declaration, was when I probably began to pick up that this war business was not a good or nice thing. It was almost certainly new routines, as well, such as actually going to the shelter, when the siren wailed that began to make an impression because it wasn't always fun. Life was going to be very, very changed in fact and I would quickly learn why and how and often I would learn in no uncertain ways, too!

I am often asked why I maintain such high interests in the subject of war, wartime, the armed forces, events and happenings of war (from the cataclysmic to the incidental if, indeed, any item of war record can be incidental) and all the written and pictorial material that there is, all devoted to this subject. My first response is, to correct the assumption that my fascination is of war per se, to the more correct attribution of the interest, which is the Second World War. Although, in some respects there is a wider inclusion by me, for instance, a continued affinity with the equipment, machinery and technology of war as it developed from this one and especially in matters aeronautical. In fact, in one of the episodes later described in my humble ramblings, there are recorded probably my earliest inklings of a passion for airplanes and, certainly, it was to be one of the main reasons for my choosing the R.A.F. in which to serve my National Service, when the time came.

Secondly, I try to explain that, for me and thousands like me, the period of World War Two was a life canvas on which our earliest impressionable, childhood memories were painted, so to speak. A big jumble of many varied events and happenings, some terrifying, some tragically emotional, some farcical, some comical but all of them telescoped into a compact period of life's experience that for others, in other times, it would take years longer to go through and, thankfully maybe, never happen. So really, my apparent fascination with war is little different from many other people, intrigued with the life and times in which they grew up and later in life wanting to add some colour, meaningful context and a deeper understanding of the background to and of their childhood days. For me such days were ones of momentous global happenings, in which ordinary civilians were thrown and, very often catapulted into, the desperate and indiscriminate consequences of war on a larger scale than ever before and which only got greater and worse. The impressions of such experiences are most certainly indelibly imprinted onto the memories of people and on those of children. For me and many others, the extent, the scope, the context and the fallout of and from those impressions, went far beyond childish innocence and naivety. Hence, in later years there has been, for me, the need for recall, for reconsideration, for acceptance even and a hint of understanding of the meaning and relevance of it all. For example, to what extent are events and people relationships of one's childhood days worked out, in the span of the following lifetime, however long or short? What influence do they really have, how does it show and for how long?

But this is not the time for philosophy, as I am on another tack and that is to record, as best my memory provides, as many of those events that are relevant to the time of war, as I can. In the past ten years or more, so many of the major players of and in my lifetime have passed away, like parents, a sister (the little sister who first features in the episode entitled, "The stuff falling on my back") grandparents, aunts, uncles and others, who were all sources of record and information, now lost because it was never written down - until now, as far as I know. So then, as with a lot of stories or writings, things begin with a title and I've called this collection of memories "Through the eyes of a child". As for the choice of title, well, not an over original one it may be said, but it was for the simplest, obvious and best of reasons that the choice was made, for me that is. I was a child, just four and a half years old almost to the day, when World War Two was declared on September 3rd. 1939 and was still one, therefore, when VE Day and VJ Day brought it all to an end almost six long, arduous years later. Was this really going to be the war to end all wars, this time?

"THE LUMP OF COAL AND TROLLEYBUS" EPISODE

This is my first obvious memory of wartime and war and my parents and I were living in Priscilla Road, Bow in East London, probably in mid-1940 after the so-called "phoney war", when nothing much happened. The air raid warning had sounded on this certain day and by the way do you, those that remember, still feel that tingle at the back of the neck whenever you hear that wailing sound? I do! It was early afternoon time, because I remember that we'd left our unfinished lunches on the table in the kitchen, when we took the headlong scramble to the Anderson shelter in the back yard, Mum, Dad and me. Following the Battle of Britain, later in 1940, the air raids were mostly at night, but this was one of the daylight raids. Whilst in the shelter, I can remember the sounds of crashing guns, the drone of airplanes, the heavier bangs of bombs dropping not far away but, far more important in my young and innocent mind, was the feeling of being hungry (my lunch was still on the kitchen table) and even more drastic, for my bladder that is, was a little boy's desperate need to do a 'wee'.

Our lavatory was the type attached to the back of the terraced house and with a door opening into the yard. Now, not 'for all the tea in China', as the saying goes, would my mother allow me to dash out of the shelter, to the lavatory and back, whilst the "raid" was still in progress – no way! As for doing it in a bucket in a corner or into a bottle or something, you just did not do that sort of thing in those days, child or not (We would soon learn otherwise!) So, there I was in agony until, at long last, the "All Clear" sounded and out I shot to the lavatory. When I opened the door of the lavatory, there on the floor in front of me, was this large piece of "something" that looked black and heavy, to me. Then, as I stood draining my over pressured bladder, I looked up to see this very large roundish, jagged hole in the roof of the lavatory. With normal bladder pressure restored and after another look at that large lump of something on the floor, I duly reported back, as my mother and father also emerged from the shelter. I said casually, "Mum, there is a big lump of coal on the floor in the lavatory and a great big hole in the roof!" Can you imagine my mother's relief at having denied me the dash to the lavatory? The big lump, as was quickly explained to me by my father, was shrapnel and not coal and, who knows, I could have been standing there in the toilet when....??

A short time later, on the same day, I went with my father up to the top of our street to the main road, to see if and where any bombs had fallen locally and what damage had been done. There, a policeman called out for my father and several other onlookers to help to push a trolleybus over the railway bridge at Bow Road station, it having lost the overhead arms and all the electric cables being down, anyway. Of course, they could not have managed it without the extra shove from a five-year-old and what fun, too. Although I was aware, by now, that episodes of war were not a good thing, such feelings as fear and danger were not yet really a part of this child's experience – it was more of a big new adventure, especially finding large lumps of coal fallen from the sky and pushing a trolleybus along! This appreciation slowly changed, as I shall comment on from time to time and as the war went on.

Almost unbelievably, the photographer of this picture, taken in the 1920's to show off the new lighting of the day, was standing at the first rise of the bridge over which we pushed the trolleybus in 1940, which would have been in the bottom right hand corner, facing this way. This picture was pre-trolleybus days – rather those of the tram, as the tracks reveal. The two tall metal posts on the right are on the corner of our road, Priscilla Road. The road is no longer there – new road, new houses!

"THE YARD SWEEPING AND DOGFIGHT" EPISODE

The timing of this flashback was certainly the summer of 1940, the Battle of Britain summer, in fact. History tells us that this battle raged until a frustrated Luftwaffe was mainly pulled off its unsuccessful attempts at annihilating the R.A.F. and switched to attacking London and other towns and cities. For me, as for many other harmless and innocent people this change was to be most significant but, for now, during those lovely summer days it was possible daily to look up into the sky and see those Spitfires, Hurricanes, Messerschmitt, Dorniers, Junkers and Heinkels, together with interlocking white trails, fighting it out and sometimes even hearing the sound of the machine gun fire, as they came lower down – dogfights they were called. Mind you, at that time, they were just airplanes to me, the names were yet to be learned, as you will read. We had moved once again (a regular occurrence as my parents struggled to get settled, in the early years of their marriage, especially with getting steady employment) and we were now back, in the block of flats in Aldgate, where my grandparents had been the Caretakers for many years. Every morning, you may recall, it was one of my Grandad's tasks to sweep the courtyard and, of course, he had that very willing and able helper. It was my special job to follow along behind and sweep up the piles of rubbish with the little shovel and into the bucket. For some reason, I can recall this day, interrupting our chores and standing, my Grandad and me, looking up into a clear blue sky to watch those airplanes, twisting and turning, leaving white trails immediately above us. Then, equally distinct in my memory is my mother's voice, coming from the open kitchen door of my grandparent's ground floor flat, calling out to both of us to come inside (I would hear her voice, on another later occasion, calling out my name but in sheer panic, not just concern!) "There may be some falling shrapnel", she said.

Can you wonder why she was so particularly sensitive about falling shrapnel? As an aside to this, little did my mother, my grandfather or me know or suspect, just how significant that patch of ground in the courtyard, on which we had stood and viewed the aerial dogfights on that sunny day, would turn out to be around three months later. That occasion would be when I would hear the sheer panic in Mum's voice, when she was calling my name, again and again. This would also be the first memorable time in my life when I know that God stepped in and protected me, yes and from death, too!

This photo of me was taken almost two years after the incident just described – I was 7 years old and it was on my Uncle Leslie's wedding day in 1942 and that's his RAF hat that I have on (the white surround in it denotes trainee aircrew) Right where I am standing, though, is about where my Grandad and I had stood and watched the 'dogfights' on that summer day in 1940! This same patch of ground would turn out to be even more significant in the October of that same year, as you will see as you read on in the next story. Note, too, that the door to the kitchen of my grandparents ground floor flat, not in shot, is no more than about 25 feet to my right as I face the camera – also significant as you will see. Lastly, I am standing right next to the base of the demolished surface shelter that once looked the same as the one in the background.

My next story will reveal how all of that came to be, on a never to be forgotten night!

"THE STUFF FALLING ON MY BACK" EPISODE

Chronology or timing is not an issue, as far as my memory is concerned in this next flashback, as I am about to describe what were probably the most momentous minutes and hours of my life, when I came as close to death as I have ever knowingly been, at the tender age of 5½ years but not that I realised that degree of significance at the time. Neither can I tell to this day, if I actually was afraid or felt afraid but I must have been and have probably blotted it out. What I can remember is what you would call bewilderment or trying to work out what was happening and as you read on, I hope that you will be able to imagine just when that bewilderment and dislike of what was taking place kicked in. As I say, when all this happened is not in question. The date is an historical fact, further verified by the dog-eared cutting from the Daily Mirror that I still have, of the report that highlighted the events of that night and the experiences of my grandparents, the family and several friends, on the night of Monday, 21st. October 1940. The detail of what happened and relevant snatches of what was said and by whom, is still crystal clear in my mind but it takes almost as long to write it down, as it took to happen and emotion overtakes me as I remember; as I relive the images, the sounds, the smells, the events and now write about, what happened.

By way of explanation and to give background to the events of that awful night, let me first explain. As described in the previous episode, which was some three months earlier, we were living in the block of flats where my grandparents had been Caretakers for many years. The Prime Minister, Winston Churchill, was to give a wireless broadcast to the nation, following the nine o'clock news, on that fateful evening. Because of this, my mother and father, my baby sister Lilian, myself, my aunt and uncle and some friends, had come down from upper floor homes in the block and were all together with my grandparents in their ground floor flat, to hear the wireless broadcast. I later understood that the air raid warning had sounded but the move to the air raid shelter, by then a nightly ritual, was delayed until the broadcast had been heard. By the way, does that not say something about the people spirit, so often reported and commented upon since, in other narratives of events of those days and times? To listen to our Prime Minister was not to be interrupted by Hitler and his bombs although me, my family and others, now desperately wish that we had so let him interfere, on this occasion!

Now, about my grandfather, he was a very quiet, private man, tall and slim, with a moustache and a rather sad but gentle face and I loved him. His favourite spot each evening was in his chair, in front of the kitchen range, the type with a hot plate, an oven, a fire with doors that you could close and all of it black and shiny, kept so by my grandmother, just as I have described elsewhere. As I learnt much later, he was, as usual, rocking my 5 months old sister to sleep, on his lap before she was put down in her pram for the night (she always slept in her pram, for the quick dashes to the shelter, I suppose?) However, she had been already settled in her pram and was not in Grandad's lap, thanks be to God and it was all because of that wireless broadcast.

The only other one in that kitchen room, one door of which opened out onto the courtyard, as described in the caption under the previous picture, was me. I was lying on the floor on my mattress bed, also already settled down, with just the long and heavy kitchen table between me and my grandfather. He was sitting in front of the fire, with his back to that courtyard door and the window alongside it. Through the other doorway that faced my grandfather, at the other end of the kitchen, was the living room. In this room was everyone else in the flat that night listening to the wireless, except my sister who was in the back bedroom. According to the recollections of the people in that living room, this was the scene a little after nine o'clock in the evening, with the news being read. I knew nothing of all this, I was usually asleep by this time and I was sound asleep that night, too, when......!

This is where my flashback starts. I clearly remember that I was kneeling, with my hands holding the bed covers tightly over my head. I hadn't heard any bang and I don't know why I was awake or in that position but again, it was my mother's voice calling my name, very panicky, that I could hear uppermost, above a lot of other noise. I called back to her, as loud as I could "Mummy, I can't get up, there is stuff falling on my back". I don't know whether she could hear me or not, but I waited until the stuff stopped falling and then I slowly raised myself up. I became even more aware of that awful noise, but I don't know what of and of people shouting and Mum still calling my name. As I threw the bedclothes back, there was this thick cloud of choking dust everywhere, but I could just make out a light shining and waving about – it was a torch in my mother's hand. She seemed to be ever so high up (perhaps clambering over rubble, I don't know) and she was still calling out to me, in that almost screaming voice, "Eddie, Eddie, where are you?" I called back to her again "I'm here, Mum" and I stood up but I had to climb over something which was in my way, was it the kitchen table or that pile of rubble, I'll never know? She grabbed hold of me and then my father was next to us and Mum was shouting, "I've got him, I've got my boy". Then she said to him, "You take Eddie, I've got to find Dad now". So, now I was in my father's arms and he was stumbling towards the kitchen doorway, presumably instinctively to try to go out into the courtyard and then, we were falling. It seems, as he described later, that he had got past where the doorway had been, taken a few steps out into where the little front garden and courtyard should have been and both of us had then tumbled straight down into a big hole, the crater left by the bomb that had fallen in the courtyard and only some 25 or so feet from our kitchen door. The significance of that fact did not dawn on me until many years later, when looking at that old photo, the one of me with my uncle's hat on. That bomb had fallen virtually on the spot, where my grandfather and I had stood and looked up at the airplanes, on that summer day some two or three months earlier. No wonder that the shelter that had been there was demolished, too. Two bombs, in fact, 250 pounders I was told, had hit our block of flats that night, one on what was called East Block, the other in the courtyard, outside the kitchen door, at most only some 30 feet or so away from where Grandad was actually sitting, and I was laying down, in the kitchen. How incredible is that? The next thing that I remember is my mother coming back, crying and saying to my father, "I can't find Dad, I've looked everywhere, we must find him, can you try?" So, once again I found myself being carried by my mother, whilst my father went off to search more for my grandfather. I have no impression of how much time elapsed between these happenings but I clearly remember a lot of noise, probably guns firing, the droning of the bombers, people shouting and someone calling out "Put that b.... light out" and someone else smashing the shining light bulb on the wall, above the entrance arch of the flats, that had lost its blackout cover. Isn't it amazing that I can so clearly remember these little incidentals and happenings?

I can then recall my father returning, saying that my uncle and grandmother were still looking for my grandfather, taking me back out of my mother's arms and then asking her, "Dearie, are you hurt? The torch he was holding showed large bloodstains on the bright yellow blouse that she was wearing but it was discovered that the blood was coming from me. I had not felt a thing but apparently, there was this lump of metal buried in my arm, up near the shoulder and the sleeve of my pyjamas was all soaked with blood. It turned out to be a piece of bomb casing and I have the two inches long scar still there today. It must have been some time later, but I remember being woken up from sleep and I was lying on this big bed with brass knobs. We had all been taken down into the underground shelter, below what was called West Block of the flats. I was so tired, but my mother made me stand up and go off with a friend of ours, Connie Doyland, an ambulance man who carried me wrapped in a blanket and a nurse, to take me to the hospital. Mum told me that she would come later when my father had come back (he was away with my uncle again still looking for my grandfather) I remember the ambulance was just a little van with a stretcher down each side and it had canvas flaps at the back, not a door and they flapped as we bumped along (another incredible detail to remember) It seemed to take ages to get to the hospital but that may have been because I kept drifting in and out of sleep or, possibly, due to having to negotiate streets blocked with rubble and fallen buildings etc.

I next remember being on a hard bed in a little cubicle and on this cabinet or table, right next to my head, was a small shiny bowl with little strips of gold coloured metal in it and some bandages. I seem to remember a nurse being there in this little room but not our friend, Connie and I wondered where she was. Where was Mum, as well, because she promised to be here, and I remember not feeling very happy with the situation at all. A Doctor made me turn over and he stuck this needle into my bottom, which set me off wailing because it hurt bad and then, there was the sound of angry voices, an awful row was going on and shouting between people. I didn't know what it was all about at the time, but it turned out to be an irate mother, who was questioning the Doctor's ability to practice his profession! Yes, it was my mother's voice again that I soon recognised. This time, she was really laying into this Doctor because he was being so rough with a child, her child. I didn't feel any more pain, though, just lying there watching the doctor start to work on my arm, stitching the wound I suppose after removing the shrapnel and…no, I don't remember anything else about that. I must have been given something to put me to sleep.

I have often tried in the many years since, especially when I started this mission of recording all that I could remember, to recall as much as I could so that a real sense of the reality of that night could be captured. Hopefully, I have been able to do that. What I am unable to do, of course, is to describe what the effects on the senses and the feelings of all my family really were. We were able to and did often talk about that dreadful night's experiences, in later years and this helped me to bring back some things that I had forgotten or, perhaps, did not want to remember. Of course, the overwhelming thing was the deep, deep sadness of the loss of my lovely grandfather, my mother's father and my grandmother's husband. I was going to miss him greatly, as he was the only grandfather that I ever had, and I was never to know him as an adult. How wonderful that one day I shall see him again, in Heaven.

However, I am able to record a personal after effect on myself! After some 70 years of knowing that I had very little hearing ability in my right ear, I just happened to mention it, whilst with my wife for her appointment with a hearing specialist and accepted the offer of an examination to see why this might be. I was promptly told that there was no mystery as to why my right ear was so lacking in hearing ability. My so-called, 'middle ear' was blown out; had no ear drum and with the fragments of the shattered little bones embedded in the roof of the ear! The first response to my question as to how that could be was, "closeness to a very loud bang, perhaps?" Can you imagine my incredulity at that answer? To think that I had accepted my poor hearing as just one of those things. It had been like it since I was 5½ years old, had happened at the explosion of the bomb that I have specifically commented that I did not hear and with little wonder! Possibly, even more surprising is, why did it go undetected at the time? Who knows?

It's claimed that 'a picture paints a thousand words' and the one that follows certainly does that for me and I will try to relay it all to the reader in less words than that! Isn't it amazing, too, how pictures and photos taken on most probably happy days, can have such poignancy in the light of subsequent events in life?

These are my grandparents standing together, just before the war, at the kitchen doorway of their ground floor flat in College Buildings – the Caretaker's flat. Note the little fence around the small front garden, with a little gate on the left and to the left of that gate was the door to the outside lavatory that I have described elsewhere. No more than about 15 feet away in front of the gated fence is the spot where the bomb landed

– the taker of this photograph is probably standing just about on that spot.

Try to visualise, too, my Grandad sitting in his chair that night by the fireplace on his right, with his back to the window and doorway that you see here, about 7 to 8 feet away, inside the kitchen. Just to his left was the long kitchen table, in the middle of the room and on the other side of which I was lying on a mattress up against the kitchen wall. Every time that I picture this scene, I cannot believe how close we were to the point of impact of that bomb! Grandad died, and I am still here to tell you about it. Is it any wonder, either, that my father fell down the crater carrying me out of the ruined kitchen and that little front garden probably also went into that crater? You can also just make out the archway at the bottom right of the picture that led through to the street and it was on the wall above this arch that the light shone that night, bereft of its blackout cover and that someone called out to extinguish. My grandmother continued to live in that flat as the Caretaker, alone, after it had been made habitable again, for the rest of the war and until she retired in 1945. The balcony above was part of the first floor flat in which Mr. & Mrs. Irwin lived, friends of my grandparents and by the way, how about all that ivy?

The events of the next day I do not clearly recall either but, apparently, we all ended up at my Aunt Lily and Uncle Bert's house in Upminster, Essex, about 15 miles east of London. I can't even remember who told me, but someone did, that Grandad had gone to heaven to be with Jesus and I was so, so upset and sad about that. Would I not be able to see him again and who would I sweep the yard with again? It transpired and in later years I learned that it had taken my father and my uncle Leslie, until halfway through that next day, touring round all the hospitals in the area before they found him, on their second visit, in the same hospital that I had been taken to, the London Hospital. He had still been alive when he reached hospital but died soon after, from serious head and multiple external and internal injuries and was so unrecognizable that, positive identification came mainly from his clothes and possessions, including his watch and chain in his waistcoat pocket. I have the confirmed report from the London Hospital that I procured many years later, which states that he had died principally from "severe laceration of the brain due to war action". That is so matter of fact and impersonal a statement, don't you think? That was my Grandad, you know, and he was only 58 years old! He'd been found by rescue workers, buried under rubble, in the doorway of that kitchen that lead into the living room and through which all those in that room listening to the wireless, had got out into the courtyard, probably trampling all over him as they did so! How had my Grandad endured and survived all that before he died? What a man! There were four other major victims that night, from the occupants of our flats, one, a family friend suffered the loss of her leg and an eye, another lost an arm, another had a serious shoulder injury and this ladies' father, had suffered chest injuries that caused his death some 2 weeks later. All these things, with all the details about what I can recall of that terrible night, are as vivid as if it were the events of last night that I was describing, as they were seen through the eyes of a child. At this point I feel that I can anticipate some reader's questioning along the lines of; why, if I was so certain that God's protection was upon my family and me during this awful event, did that protection not extend to my grandfather? Well, for one reason, it is not for me to question God's purpose and will for anyone but, secondly, I believe that it was God's time to take my grandfather, as we all have a time to pass on from this life. I know, too, that God had something better for Grandad, which was not to be found on this earth but in Heaven.

This is a modern day picture of the London Hospital and the drinking fountain that I remember so well. There is now a helipad on the roof! When I contacted the archivist here, to seek copies of my grandfather's and my own admittance records I learnt that the hospital, only about a mile or so away from us, had also been hit by bombs on the same night as we had - how chaotic must that have been and a wonder that any casualties were attended to!

"THE GREEN CUSHION" EPISODE

This next flashback memory is centred at the scene of the loss of my dear grandfather and again only some 7 months later. The dating of it I can yet again be sure of, having been told that it was on what has later been deemed as the worst night of that seemingly endless battering of London, known as the 'Blitz' and that was Saturday, May 10th. 1941. Incidentally, I have since discovered that this day was FA Cup Final day, as well, with Arsenal playing Preston North End, Tom Finney and all! However, that was some 5 years before I myself became an avid and active supporter of the 'Gunners'. So, to continue, some weeks after the loss of my grandfather, my grandmother, insisting on continuing as the Caretaker of the flats, moved back into her repaired home with the boarded-up windows and did just that, carried on but now on her own. Again, this attitude was so typical of Londoners and others, in cities and towns, suffering personal loss and in many other ways but portraying that indomitable spirit, which was about the only thing remaining in good supply, in those dark and dangerous days. As I have already recorded about other episodes, the events that took place on this night and the next day are just as vivid and fresh in my mind, as if they had happened only yesterday. Maybe, in this case, they were burned into my memory, as you'll see? Again, it was to be an occasion when I am convinced that God protected me, other members of my family and my Dad, no question!

Following on from the destruction of our home, commonly known as "being bombed out", my father insisted on us moving out of Central London. So, I stayed on with my mother's sister, in my aunt and uncle's house in Upminster, about 15 miles away at the far end of the District Line of the London Underground, for the time being – I suspect that my aunt insisted on that! My mother and sister were evacuated to Swindon in Wiltshire, a few weeks later but I cannot remember whether my father joined them there or not, before he was called up into the Army. I remember that they were with an older couple in the centre of Swindon at first but moved to a suburb called Pinehurst, where I was to join them later. After a period of several months, my parents decided that I should be joined up with my mother and my sister again. So, my father, who had been called up by now in January 1941 and was stationed, in the Army, at Blandford in Dorset, obtained weekend leave to come and take me from Upminster to Swindon and that was on that day May 10th. 1941. So, of course, having to come back into Central London, from Upminster to get to Paddington station, meant that I just had to pay a visit to my two doting grandmothers, both of whom would not hear of their grandson passing by without calling in to see them, especially with him going so far away and not knowing when they might see him next. It was an opportunity, too, for my father to see his mother and mother-in-law before he went overseas, as he surely would soon, because that was the natural process after being drafted into the forces.

Firstly then, to my father's mother in Bow where we had to stay and have something to eat, of course. Then, before she would allow us to leave to go to my other grandmother, there had to be the usual "quick drink" in the pub at the top of the street, with her son, before he went off back to his Army barracks and then on to wherever. She always liked her stout and another EastEnders's favourite drink – mild and bitter! I seem to remember that it was around late afternoon or teatime and we still had to go to the home of my other grandmother. With strictly no children in the pubs in those days, I had to wait outside, and I remember sitting on the upraised wooden hatchway cover, over the cellar entrance, down through which the beer barrels were passed from the street when the brewer's dray came calling to top up supplies. After a while my father and grandma came out and she handed me a tiny glass, telling me to "drink it all up, son, it'll warm the cockles of yer 'eart, for the long journey". It was vile stuff and must have been a tot of brandy or whisky and she was most insistent that I drink it up – oh, the joys of grandmother's potions! Of course, I did not finish it all up and after the usual tearful goodbyes, we left one grandmother to go to the other and by now it was already getting well on towards the evening. The following picture is taken outside that same pub many years later and it was still there when I passed by in October 2006. It was strange thinking back to that evening some 65 years earlier – a lifetime!

"The Caledonian Arms" at the top of Blondin Street where my grandmother lived. It must have been some club outing and in the picture are my Uncles, Alf, he's the second from the left at the back and Charlie, he's the tenth from the left also at the back. On the far right of the picture, there is a doorway to the pub and just to the right of this is the hatchway, obscured by the group, on which I sat that May evening in 1941 whilst Dad and Nan had their drinks inside.

We left to go back, in fact, to the very same flat in College Buildings in Aldgate, where we had lost my grandfather and I had stopped my bomb splinter only some 7 months earlier! Sadness again, for me, as I again remembered all about my grandad, who wasn't there anymore, and it was emotional sitting in the same room, like it used to be when he was around.

The blown down kitchen door had been replaced but the little front garden was no longer there. The shattered windows were boarded up and the ruined kitchen had been repaired and redecorated and we sat in that same kitchen, beside the same range fireplace, at the same table to eat – the big sturdy one that was between me and my grandfather on the night of the bombing. So, this grandmother wasn't going to let her only grandson go all the way off to Swindon either, at night as well, without some good hot soup inside of him. There then, the maternal instincts of my two doting grandmothers, brandy (or some such thing) from the one and soup from the other and I remember struggling with both – one too bitter and the other too hot! What I didn't realize but my father probably did, was that the time was getting late and we had quite a long journey, on the Underground to get to Paddington station to catch the mainline train. After the struggle with the hot soup we finally left with hardly enough time to make it and we first had to catch the Underground train at Aldgate East station. We stopped and started all the way to Paddington and, sure enough, we missed that mainline Swindon train – by just minutes! I can still picture the anxiety, disappointment and worry on my father's face and the long conversation with the Ticket Collector at the ticket barrier, as to whether there was some other train or way to get to Swindon that night. But no, not on a Saturday night and so, there was nothing for it but to run quickly back to the Underground, to return home to Gran's before those trains, too, stopped for the night. I am not sure about what time the train was that we missed, probably around 9.30pm or what time it was when we got back to my grandmother's place but I think we were just in time to catch her before she retired for the night, into a nearby shelter, situated in the basement of a large office block, immediately behind our flats, called Toynbee Hall. The Air Raid warning had sounded on our way back from Paddington so we, of course, went with her and I remember being tucked down in a bed of sorts but nothing more, as I went into the sleep of an exhausted 6 year old, blissfully unaware of the more dramatic events that were to follow, on another and, as history would confirm, the most dreadful night of the Blitz.

Well into the night, it must have been in the early hours, I was awakened by my father, as everyone was being evacuated from the shelter. We were told that both the building above us and others surrounding it were ablaze, that the incendiary fires were getting out of control and so the order to evacuate to another shelter had been passed down. We went up the several flights of stairs to the ground floor, shepherded all the way by Air Raid Wardens and out of the back door of the building, into the rear yard. I'll never ever forget the sight that greeted us! It was just awful and unbelievably terrifying, especially for a small boy. It was as bright as noonday in the middle of the night, except that the light was created not by the sun or the moon but by fires, dozens and dozens of them! All around us almost every building was on fire and burning, including the upper floors of the building above us and the basement shelter of which we were leaving. We were told which other shelter we were being taken to, which was only a short walk away down an alley between the buildings, but this alley was impassable because of the fires. So, we were led out of the yard, into a back street and we had to do a left detour around the block, which took us back past the front entrance to my grandmother's flats. The air, I clearly remember was stifling hot, it was difficult to breathe and everywhere there were flying sparks and glowing debris floating down. Strangely, our block of flats seemed to be escaping the fires, although only the courtyard separated them from a blazing building behind them and a narrow alley from another building next to them, also on fire. Yet, we still dashed indoors for my grandmother to pick something up and I clearly recall what it was – a large cushion from off the armchair and it was green in colour a very light green. What for, you might well ask? You'll see!

As we came out into the courtyard again, to get back out onto the street, something else I remember (yet another of those amazing incidentals that are still so, so clear) was the sight of blistering, crackling paint. You see, the big, wooden door to the office, next to my grandmother's flat (remember, the weekly rents were collected in this office) was only about 30 to 40 feet away from the other side of the yard and the wall of that building that was burning so fiercely. The heat was so intense from the flames that the chocolate brown paint on the door was blistering, crackling and hissing and the reflection of the flames danced on the paint and I can see it all, even now and, I can smell it, too! All of us could feel the heat and that's when that big, bright green cushion was plonked on my head, with the instruction to hold it there as just a protection of sorts from all the swirling sparks and glowing embers drifting down in clouds. So, along we went to the exit from our courtyard, through the arch under West Block, turned left out into Wentworth street, some 30 yards or so up to the corner and turned left again into Commercial Street to complete the round the block detour, going back past the building from under which we had been evacuated and so making our way to the safer shelter that we had been directed to but not as simply as it sounds to tell it!

Once more the sight that greeted us, as we turned that last corner into Commercial Street, was hard to take in and is just as hard for me to now describe, because of its horror, all these years later. How can I put into words what I saw, adequately enough, to convey the effect of such a sight on anybody, let alone a six-year-old boy? There was fire pouring out of the roofs and windows of every building, on each side of the road; the spray from the hoses of the fire engines was coming down like rain, the sparks and cinders were keeping pace with the spray, there was this awful burning smell and the choking smoke, endless piles and mounds of bricks and rubble from collapsed walls over which to try and scramble to progress along the street and then there was water, water and more water! We were almost up to our knees in it, each time we stumbled up, over and down a mound of rubble and we then splashed into the water. How my grandmother managed the clambering over the rubble, I really cannot say but my father probably helped her. Then over and above all of this mayhem there was the bewildering, terrifying, mind numbing noise. The combined racket and din of roaring fires, loud exploding bombs, guns firing, falling masonry, fire engines and water pumps, firemen shouting and whatever else was absolutely deafening – hellish, even! In fact, just how we all succeeded in doing the 200 yards or so along Commercial Street, until we reached the entrance to the alternative deep underground shelter, or how long it took us to do it, I have no idea but, finally, we did. It was situated at the Aldgate end of Commercial Street, opposite what was then Woolworths and almost at the junction of Aldgate High Street, in what was called Essex Yard. In the shelter, I remember this long, long corridor with bunks all along one wall and I think I ended up on a top one, because I was looking down watching others of my family and some friends gradually congregating together, from other parts of the shelter. There was my Uncle Leslie's fiancé, her sister and mother and lots of people from all around the neighbourhood. All of us were tired, battered, filthy, wet up to the knees or waist even and fearful as to whether we were going to see the night through safely. Would the fires be brought under control or would they spread to threaten and endanger us again, would we be herded out for a second time into those terrifying streets? These were just some of the questions racing through everyone's minds, with no real answers available from or for anyone, just resignation! Just pray!

Then I slept again, long and we all then emerged from down there, well into the "daylight" of the next day, when it was adjudged safe for us to do so. Once more, the image and the scenes that greeted us are clear for me, not really like daylight at all and unforgettable. It was dull, miserable and very black and white in my memory with absolutely no colour. What we had seen in the dark hours of the beginning of that day, by the light of fires, we now saw in sombre, smoky, greyish daylight. What had been a multi-coloured scene to the eye, with flames roaring noisy and explosive, smoke threatening to overwhelm us and very, very frightening, now had many of the same characteristics but with no colour at all, just black and white or grey to look at. There was much, much less noise as a lot of the fires were either nearly out or under control, the bombing and gun firing noises had ceased and the panic of harm and danger was now replaced by a dread or fear that our home would not be still standing, because the buildings around were all now largely skeletons of walls and still smoking or burning. The piles and mounds of bricks and rubble were there still, perhaps bigger; they had to be clambered over again, the water still had to be waded through, but the "rain" of spray was not so bad and the clouds of sparks and burning debris was much reduced. The scene was awful and depressing, stark, chaotic looking, foul smelling and, I say again, very black and grey with no colour at all. This is what we made our way through and past and over, on that round the block detour again, to get back to my grandmother's flats and as we came around the last corner we looked and yes, they were still standing and amazingly, unharmed this time. You see, God had spared us and kept us safe despite the awfulness of that night. There was no water, no electricity and no gas in the flat, mind you and I cannot remember what we did about all that. Knowing my Gran, she probably conjured up something or perhaps one of the mobile kitchens came to the rescue with a hot drink and sandwiches, but I cannot remember.

This is the Aldgate end of Commercial Street and the shop on the right-hand corner, used to be Woolworths. The shelter into which we all filed, in the event just recorded, was in Essex Yard laying back behind the low building on the left, now in its place. The view straight down Commercial Street exactly covers the '200 yards or so' of my narrative and takes the eye down to just beyond the tall block, on the left. Wentworth Street, out of which we emerged after our detour, entered Commercial Street from the right at this point. Evidence of the devastation caused by those fires that night is that all of the buildings on the left, from this foreground corner, down past and including the very tall block, are new erections since the war, as are those on the opposite side and the road has been widened along that whole stretch, too! From this corner we walked towards the right, going left at the next turning and then left again, to bring ourselves back into our street, climbing piles of rubble, wading through water and past smoking ruins.

Late in the afternoon of that next day, the Sunday, some 80 miles or so away from the scenes that I remember so well and have described, my mother was, by now, quite frantic with worry, anxiously awaiting news, just any news but fearful of what that news might be. No doubt, something of the previous night's events engulfing East London had filtered through over the wireless. No mobile 'phones and most houses had no landline 'phones, either, in those days. Where were her husband and son, were they safe? We, my father and me, should have arrived in Swindon the previous evening and my mother had neither heard nor seen anything from or of us and had no inkling of what had really happened, only her worst fears and nightmares of the wartime days in which we lived. She told us afterwards that she had stood despairingly at the window for hours that morning after a sleepless night, looking and waiting but no sight of her husband and son. Then, unexpectedly and well into the afternoon, there was a knock at the door of the house where my mother and sister were billeted and she rushed to the door (as she often told later) to be greeted by these two scruffy, filthy, dirty individuals, one a man and the other a small boy and they looked remarkably like a chimney sweep and his lad – me and my Dad! The journey down from London I cannot remember, but I do remember being greeted by an incredulous mother, being very tired, hungry and eating, then feeling even more tired and going to bed and well, whatever happened then I don't remember.

EVACUATION BLUES

Evacuation, now there's a term. It meant being separated from your mother and father, removed from your home and transported endless miles away from the city in which you lived or if your home was in a location deemed to be too dangerous for children to remain. You ended up, often split from your brother or sister, in homes of strangers, in places mostly quite diverse to what you were used to or even knew existed. Some kids from the confines of city slum life, who may have known of cows and sheep but had never seen one in the flesh, were plonked on a farm where you practically lived with them! This government scheme implemented almost as soon as war was declared was appropriately called 'Operation Pied Piper'. My sister and I were of the luckier ones, who were uplifted and deposited together with our mother but that did not make the experience any better for us. As it transpired, my mother did not get on very well with the people that we were, as it was called, billeted with in Pinehurst, Swindon or more correctly, with the wife and mother of the family. I am sure that this must have been the case with many other similar scenarios, brought about by these emergency procedures of the government of the day. Many families and children managed the upheaval superbly, but many failed to adjust to the sometimes quite dramatic change in lifestyle. Complete strangers were thrown together, in times of enormous strain on every family in the land, let alone the added social, practical and interactive stresses involved in sharing households. We were often later reminded, by my mother, about the selfish and unreasonable treatment from the lady of the house where we were billeted. This was in contrast to the more understanding attitude of the husband, who was very domineered by his wife, however. Then there was the couple's only child, a daughter aged about 10 and who was blameless and of impeccable behaviour, or so her mother was convinced or claimed but who was actually selfish, spoilt and quite dislikeable! All in all, not a social mix that stood much chance of lasting amicably for very long, only about 8 months for us, in fact, which is quite good, really. It was long enough, in any event, for me to have a couple of memorable episodes with painful outcomes to recount, one for me and one for my kid sister, now round about one year old or so.

"THE STICK AND STONES" EPISODE

For me the root cause of my pain was truancy and, therefore deserved but at the same time to be understood. Basically, and I suppose, for the obvious reasons, I was not very happy living in or going to school in Swindon. I believe that it had a great deal to do with being a Cockney Londoner and not fitting in with the lifestyle or attitudes of country folk and I probably picked up on my mother's discontent, too. So, I remember one day bunking off school with this other boy and roaming the streets of Tilehurst, the district of Swindon where we lived. It was on a lovely summer day and we sat on the kerbside of one of the roads, in the afternoon sun, just idly throwing stones bouncing along the roadway. In those days and in wartime, too, not many cars were on the roads, but the inevitable one did come along and approached the spot where we were just playing. Well now, the monotony of bouncing stones along the road, suddenly became potentially much more exciting – we could bounce those stones off this moving target, couldn't we? We both agreed about that and carried out the dastardly deed, quickly followed by a dramatic dash from the scene of the crime and all was well, and the rest of the afternoon went pleasantly by!

I duly arranged to be home at about the time that I would normally so be from school and all was still well. Until, that is, the knock on the door that heralded the arrival of some officious character, who had not called for the benefit of my health or wellbeing but I, nevertheless, was the object of the call! Who it was, maybe the car owner of the afternoon prank or someone from my school, I knew not. I clearly remember the consequences, though, starting with the question from Mum "Have you been to school, today?" The rest of the interrogation was just a blur really, I can't even remember what I said to defend myself. I just knew that I was soon to be in one heap of trouble and my diagnosis was very accurate. It all ended up with me running up the stairs towards the sanctuary of the bedroom, hotly and expertly pursued by my stick wielding, very angry mother, laying into the backs of my legs with a considerable degree of success. There was much wailing and gnashing of teeth that evening on my part and, I recall, much sadness too, that I had caused my mother to get so mad with me. She was very, very upset, as well and I can remember her crying with me. I think that the pressure that she was obviously suffering under had got to her and she regretted that she had, what we would call in today's parlance, lost the plot. Poor Mum, I believe that she knew in her heart of hearts that her son was non-too happy with life there either. The next day mother escorted me (I wonder why?) into school and we ended up together in the Headmistress's room and another dressing down came my way. When my mother had departed, I was left in the room with this old dragon of a Headmistress and her first act was to confiscate my pack of sandwiches that Mum always gave me to take to school. She could not have done a crueller act and I had this wicked almost overwhelming urge to give her one enormous kick in the leg but, somehow, I laid hold of myself and contented myself with just hating her – intensely! You see, an abiding memory of any part of those wartime days, for me, was always being hungry. Not because I was starved, but nobody was overfed, and boys are always hungry even in times of plenty. The sight of my lovely sandwiches being taken away was a body blow – literally. Anyway, probably because I resisted my evil urge to lash out, I am here today as the writer of this tale of "sticks and stones" memories!

"THE FINGER TRAPPING" EPISODE

So, to that other painful episode that I mentioned, but this time the pain was for my sister, Lilian. It must have been some time later, maybe a couple of months or so and it involved that very spoilt and mischievous daughter of the family where we stayed, whose name escapes me. Being not much more than a year or so old, my sister spent quite a lot of time sitting in her pram, playing with her toys etc. It was the old-style pram with the big wheels, big curved handle and the large hood that pulled right up high. On this day, I had come home from school and was sitting in the lounge or front room, as we called it then, reading a comic, I think. My mother was in the kitchen helping the lady of the house to prepare the evening meal and my sister was sitting in her pram as I have described also in the lounge, beside the open door. The hood of the pram was folded down flat, to be out of the way except that this nuisance of a daughter kept pulling the hood up and then closing it down again, up and down, up and down. I clearly heard my mother, looking through from the kitchen, repeatedly asking and then loudly telling the girl, to stop playing with the hood of the pram or she would trap the baby's fingers, between the metal surround of the hood and the side of the pram. That's right, you can guess that the inevitable did happen. Up went the hood, baby sister's fingers clasped the side of the pram and down came the hood again, not very gently and there were the little fingers, quite badly squeezed, bloodied and bruised. My mother went ballistic, in today's vernacular and the resultant head to head clash, of the respective parents was terminal, in terms of my mother staying there, in that house any longer. It was real "skin and hair" flying stuff, figuratively speaking and covered every aspect of being a woman, wife, mother, creature and then some. The pent-up emotions, frustrations and indignity of being treated as ignorant "townies", as well, just boiled over. You can just imagine that she had some choice home truths already for the husband to be treated to, when he came home from work, as well. For instance, advice suggesting a change to wearing certain feminine clothing that would be much more appropriate for him, as he most certainly did not wear the trousers in the house! The poor man was swept aside as he tried to "pour oil onto troubled waters", as the saying goes. He was already hen-pecked by his wife and was certainly and utterly blown away by my mother in full cry. The very next day we were, the three of us, packed up and on our way back to London, never to be officially evacuated again. For my mother and my sister, it was to see the rest of the war out staying in London, moving from the flats where my grandmother soldiered on as Caretaker, to another top floor 3 roomed flat in the world famous Petticoat Lane, just a few streets away. This flat turned out to be our family home for long after the war, when my father came home from Army service overseas and my other sister duly arrived, quite soon actually and all five of us then lived in those 3 rooms - those were the days! The record of them features much later in my memoirs, when I was to return home to London, my father was to return from the war and so for us all to be a family once more. For me, after Swindon, it was off back to live with my aunt and uncle, in Upminster as before, for the rest of the war and I have some vivid recollections of those days, as well and here they are recorded in the following pages.

MY WARTIME HOME

My aunt and uncle's house was semi-detached, with a small front garden and a long, narrow rear one, in a quiet suburban style street about half a mile from the focal point of Upminster, the crossroads where the local road junctioned with the main one to London and noted by being the site of 'The Bell' pub. Back in those days, it was far more rural than is the case today and was deemed to be by us Londoners as, in the country, or so we termed it. It was also rather "posh" and I distinctly remember that certain attitude, to put it nicely, towards me as a poor kid from East London. Belittling and patronising, I began to find it really, as I got older and noticed and felt it more. This was not from my relatives, of course, but was evident to me from some neighbours, locals and most especially at school. For instance, "What, you haven't got a bathroom or a garden?" type question. However, this apart, I have only very fond and happy memories of this period of my childhood and despite being in a very strict religious regime, as my relatives all followed the faith of Plymouth Brethren. This is not the place, however, for debating upon such details, I just insert them here and there as background, although I am eternally grateful for the influence and effect on my life, of this Christian background and upon which I shall expand later.

This is a 2007 picture of the modernized version of the house in Upminster, the centre one. The windows and front door are original – just repainted, the front door now black. The small front garden is concreted over, and the low wooden fence removed to park a car. Just above the house to the left, can be seen one of the lines of tall trees that stretched across the bottom of each rear garden and over which screamed those German airplanes, on that summer morning, in my story that you'll read later.

So, I'll relate some more flash backs and memories of events that left their impression. Before that, the photos below show, on the left, the Brethren meeting hall that the family attended every Sunday, just up the road from our house. The second is taken in the rear garden in Upminster, probably around 1939 and is again interesting in identifying the sites and locations of the things that can add illustration to my stories. As an aside, too, as with me you can probably sense that "apple of her eye" feel, in my Aunt's stance, in the photo, that I have commented on elsewhere?

This first photo, on the left, is of me in 2005 outside the hall that we attended on Sunday for our Christian services.

The second is a remarkable photo because, a great big hole was dug into the ground, to locate the partly sunken Anderson Shelter (next picture) that features in one of my later stories and was right where my Aunt is sitting with me. In the centre background, too, is one of the line of trees that I talk about in the story entitled "Tip and run raid". Finally, just to the right and behind both of us, stood our tree in the line and around which all those rabbit hutches were built, that I tell you about later, too.

An Anderson Shelter. This is not our one or me for that matter! Our one was covered by a greater depth of earth and plants, shrubs etc plus a small porch across the front, covering the entrance door. Inside was lots of straw, blankets, bunks, chairs, an oil lamp and paraffin heater – it was still cold in winter and damp from condensation.

"THE SMELL IN THE SHELTER" EPISODE

My uncle was a C.O. (Conscientious Objector) meaning that he was exempted from military service and in his case, it was on religious grounds. However, it also meant that he had to do other service and he chose to be an Air Raid Warden in the A.R.P. and the Post that he reported to was just a short walk away, in the next street. He would go on duty most nights of the week and my aunt and I would go into the shelter whenever the siren went, again, most nights of the week, so I would probably date this as around late 1941, after I had returned from being evacuated to Swindon. What is known as 'the Blitz' was still ongoing but at a reduced intensity, although raids were a regular occurrence. Anyway, more for the sake of company, we used to often go into the shelter of the Tyler family next door, with my friend, Jimmy and his mother, especially when Mr. Tyler was working on late shift – he was an engine driver. At this point, let me explain what the shelters were in terms of the personal safety of the population. The shelter, for many, was an Anderson shelter, like the one in the picture just seen. At the outbreak of war every household was issued with one for siting in the rear garden or yard, made of sheets of corrugated iron half buried into a large, rectangular shaped hole that you dug about three feet into the ground and the curved roof, about three feet above ground level, was covered over with a deep layer of earth and whatever else one chose to heap onto it. If you were not blessed with a rear garden or yard your issue was a Morrison shelter, which was a large steel mesh cage with a thick steel sheet on the top, under which it was intended for the family to shelter or sleep during the air raids. Most families had them in the living room and used the top as a table, instead of the kitchen or dining table. In the event of the house being demolished on top of you, survival under the Morrison shelter was reckoned to be long enough for rescue workers to dig you out. The Anderson shelter in the garden was relatively safe unless falling foul of a direct hit. Indeed, families were known to have emerged from their Anderson shelter after the 'all clear' siren in the morning, only to discover that some of the bangs and crashes of the night's raids were, in fact, their own house being flattened, maybe only twenty or thirty yards away! It's interesting to note that the issue of either type of shelter was free, provided that the household income was £250 per annum or less. If it was more than £250 then the shelter had to be purchased - for £7. Our Anderson shelter, at the bottom of our back garden, was concrete lined to just above the ground level, which helped to eliminate the biggest drawback of the Anderson, severe damp or even flooding. There were small steps down into our one, through a stout wooden door with a small porch that protected the entrance on those rainy nights. The whole area inside was about seven feet by five feet and you could just about stand up, if of an average height. The furnishings and fittings depended entirely upon ingenuity and skill but were largely biased towards sleeping comfort and making hot drinks as best could be achieved, although, such standards varied considerably, largely commensurate with the family's D.I.Y. capabilities.

So, now to the night in question and that of my story. My uncle was on duty and we were in the shelter with Jimmy Tyler and his mother. Jimmy was younger than me and was asleep in his bunk and I remember being half asleep myself, on another bunk but being woken up by Mr. Tyler, returning from his shift and clambering down into the shelter. He settled straight down into his old armchair, rolled and lit a cigarette and soon went to sleep, starting to snore. It was not long after that I began to get the whiff of a strange and unpleasant smell. Now, you know the innocence of a child will always have its way and I can still hear myself, to this day saying "Aunt, there is a terrible bad smell in here!" You can imagine the reaction from her and shall we just say that it was a rather strongly put suggestion that I keep quiet. After a while I insisted, "But, Aunt, it is a really bad smell, can't you smell it?" Another strong whispered command that meant that I should put a sock in it and now. I needed third party help, so I then asked Mrs. Tyler "Can you smell a bad smell in here, Mrs. Tyler?" which did not result in a very clear reply but there was more persistent encouragement from my aunt to choke or something but to shut up about the smell. No way, it was really a nasty smell. "I can still smell it, you know", I reminded her a little later.

How long this exchange of innocent, childlike insistence and dogged adult dismissal went on for, I cannot recall but I do know that it was decided that it was time for us to return to the sanctuary (for my aunt) of our own shelter. However, as is often the case in life, other purely coincidental happenings have a bearing on proceedings and, in this case, it was quite comical. Just as we were making our way from one back garden to the other, a local battery of ack ack guns (anti-aircraft) opened up with a deafening racket and we were both galvanized into a mad charge for our shelter, in case of falling shrapnel. Down the side passage of the house we ran with me in the lead, across the concrete patio, then over the lawn and straight down the little steps of the porch. I slammed open the door of the shelter and jumped headlong onto the big double bed, quickly followed by my aunt. Well, we both landed full tilt on top of my uncle, sound asleep on the mattress and we frightened the living daylights out of him. It transpired that, he had been sent off duty early and not wishing to disturb us, thinking we would be asleep in the shelter next door, he had settled on the mattress for a sleep himself and then the world fell in on him.   Oh, and that smell that I was severely chastised for keeping on about was real and my Aunt was just as nauseated by it, too but could not say that she knew what it was all the time. Apparently, Mr. Tyler was quite a drinker and on his way home from work, his habit was to call into the pub for several pints with his mates. In the confined space of the shelter and with the relaxed helplessness of sleep, the combination of beery breath, stale cigarette and the passing of smelly wind was a pretty obnoxious cocktail of odour. What would an innocent young lad know about such things and I had only asked what the funny smell was. Somehow, my aunt had managed to extricate us both from the highly embarrassing episode but in doing so, had then run us both into the coincidence of the guns opening on enemy raiders, a mad scamper to reach our shelter, the hurried dive through the doorway and my uncle comically but painfully suffering the consequences.

AERONAUTICAL STIRRINGS!

Without doubt, in most people's minds, an extremely defining chapter in Second World War history, was the aerial conflict aptly named "The Battle of Britain". Whatever the passage of time and the often doubtfully attributed "benefit" of hindsight, that some commentators of history may have us believe, the fact remains that if the result of that battle had been any other than what it was, our world would now be a totally different place and how.   For me, my world was different, anyway, even with the resultant victory of that battle because, just a few short weeks after that battle, when the bombing raids started on London, I had lost my Grandad, I had been slightly injured and that made things very, very sadly different.

Ironically, Upminster, where I had finally ended up again some 9 months after that loss, was a mere 3 miles from one of the most crucially important airfields of the Battle of Britain campaign, the RAF station at Hornchurch. That battle was already recent history, but the airfield continued to be a major part of the defensive shield protecting London and the South East and activity there was constant and daily. As the war progressed, of course, the squadrons based there, went onto the offensive and flying business, if anything, increased even more.

I believe that this nearness to the perpetual hustle and bustle of that fighter station plus another influence, was the beginning of what blossomed into a life-long interest, for me, in airplanes. The other influence referred to, stemmed from my father serving in the Royal Artillery, stationed on an anti-aircraft gun site and his being responsible for aircraft recognition, in his gun crew. Whenever I saw him home on leave, in the first few months of his service, he would bring me one of those little books that looked just like the old Penguin paperbacks. They were the official Army training manuals on aircraft recognition, with photos, plan silhouettes, specifications and all the performance details, on every military aircraft in service, both friendly and enemy. Whether or not I should have been in possession of these books I know not and cared even less, because they were like treasures to me, with many hours spent poring over and assimilating the information. Of course, with such close proximity to the often, low flying, real examples of the book's contents, I progressed to become quite an accomplished spotter myself. As the war dragged on the familiar British aircraft types were supplemented by American machines, with Essex and the other East Anglian counties being home base to many bomber and fighter escort squadrons. There were also other types, training and transport, to be seen in the Essex skies, all identified with the help of my little books from Dad. The experience of "seeing" any German planes, though, was always limited to on a, too high to clearly make out basis, mostly in dog-fights on a clear day (I was never fortunate to get to an enemy plane crash site before the demolition crews cleared everything away, to see even a broken one close up) But, even this was to change in a dramatic, pulse racing fashion, as a later episode will describe, with real, live and nasty German airplanes and very, very close to boot!

COLLECT AND KEEP!

One of the habitual characteristics of boys, over the ages, has been an addiction to collecting things and these times of war introduced all sorts of new and exciting things to search for, collect and hoard. A lot of those "collectables" came out of the skies, like my lump of "coal" of earlier days, more correctly named, shrapnel. This was mostly the fragments of shattered shell casings, after exploding thousands of feet up and falling to the ground, ready to be found and hoarded. Sometimes, it was the nose cone of an Ack Ack shell and sometimes, highly dangerously, even a whole unexploded shell. Then there were "spent" bullet and or cannon shell casings, from an aircraft's armament and, again, some of the unhealthy unexploded variety. Finally, and equally highly prized, were pieces of actual aircraft fallen off in combat and scattered over the countryside or the "trophies" recovered from crashed wreckages, with those from enemy planes the most coveted. Amongst my collection, in two wooden boxes, were various small pieces of wings or fuselages, a pitot head (that's an aircraft's air speed measuring device) lots of clips and casings from machine gun bullets and two highly treasured items; an oxygen bottle from a German bomber, a Dornier 17, I believe, with real German writing on it and a live cannon shell, probably 20mm, from I know not what gun – friend or foe.

Quite late in the war, I remember somehow gaining access, with a couple of mates, to the site of a crashed American B.17 bomber – a Flying Fortress, no less. From memory, I think that the aircraft had crash landed some time before returning damaged from a bombing raid, that most of the wreckage had been recovered and taken away and the site left with nobody to deny access, after the initial guard, except the farmer on whose land it had happened. Of course, he had little or no chance against such determined and agile hunters of interesting things to collect, as us lads. We had a ball, as they say and I remember several expeditions resulting in lots of booty being recovered but because it became too large an amount of stuff to take to our homes, we established a secret dump. Many a weekend afternoon or summer evening was spent thereafter, discussing what the various scraps were and happily bargaining and swapping with friends, in our secret hideaway. My uncle was somewhat of a collector, too, very often bringing home his finds from the many gardens and allotments that he worked on.

STORIES OF FOOD, RATIONING AND THE "BLACK MARKET"

Some of the abiding memories of my wartime days are not always filled with tragedy, drama, comedy or even emotion but are just interesting, so to speak, as gauges of the atmosphere and the attitudes that prevailed, with their impact on everyday living and lives. I have recorded elsewhere for instance, in another story, about an abiding memory of always being hungry. Food was, always has been and always will be, a serious part of life and a matter very high on a boy's agenda, especially when scarce. From some aspects I was fortunate, in that I probably enjoyed some benefits that others did not, as was the case with other "country folk". You see, my uncle's daily occupation was a gardener, self-employed and he had a considerable clientele of people's gardens to tend and upkeep, as well as maintaining a biggish "allotment" of his own. An allotment was a parcel of land upon which you grew your own produce and ours, with many others, was on the local golf course now given over to such wartime circumstances, as well as all sorts of training and other activities of the Army. This all meant that we were recipients of any gifted surplus of uncle's gardening clients, plus the crops harvested from our own allotment. Now, in addition to this, in our back garden, we kept some fifty to sixty rabbits, which provided both extra income from sales to neighbours etc, for my aunt and uncle and also supplemented the almost non-existent meat content of our meagre war rationed diet. So, here are several episodes that involve or centre on, the subject of food and firstly, those rabbits. In relation to the subject of food, though, here are two pictures that illustrate the Ration Book and, for interest sake, an Identity Card. I was not to become too familiar with the Ration Book until after the war, when I returned home and began to run errands for Mum, although I remember going with my aunt to the Food Office to collect our new ration books when needed. Back home in London, many were the times when I was dispatched to Hetty's, our little Jewish grocer with a request from Mum, for a quarter pound of tea, a pound of sugar, some butter or cheese maybe, off next week's ration. Maybe even, for a little extra money and to save the coupons we would get it on the "black Market!"

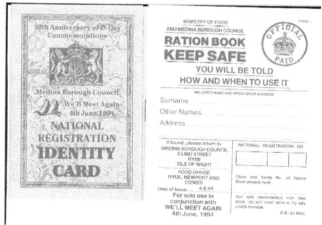

These are not originals, but copies printed for the 60th. Anniversary celebrations, however, they are true copies. The Identity Card always had to carried with you. The Ration Book had several pages and was either marked with indelible pencil or had coupons torn out, as your nominated grocer supplied the goods. Everything was either dated or week numbered, too.

I will describe, initially, where and how we managed to keep all the rabbits that I have just referred to. At the bottom of our garden, about thirty yards from the house stood a tall elm tree, with a big, round, firm base and was one of a straight line of six, all at the end of other gardens either side of us. Around the base of this tree and across the back fence of the garden, were stacked rows of rabbit hutches, with two or three occupants in each. In front of this "colony", to separate it from the domestic part of the garden was a glass greenhouse, but which had a wooden door. Incidentally, in front of the greenhouse was the Anderson shelter that features in another story, elsewhere. Feeding the rabbits was a daily chore, in which I was very enthusiastically involved, although one part of that process, exclusively mine, was a real pain as a chore and cleaning out was none too pleasant, either. Anyway, my uncle had this very large round, quite shallow, cast iron bowl with handles on each side. Early each morning all sorts of vegetable waste, potato peelings, storks from Brussel sprouts, greenery from the tops of carrots, turnips, parsnips etc were all chopped up in this large bowl, using the sharp edge of a garden spade. Into this was added an ample measure of bran, a quantity of hot water and the whole concoction mixed up with the same spade, as if you were mixing cement. This was then shared out in separate bowls and put into each hutch, plus a bowl of water and that was the main meal of the day, for the rabbits, that is.

However, each evening, they were given hay and other greenery to munch and this was the chore that gave me such grief. It wasn't the feeding part, which I never minded but the procurement of this feed, which I loathed. Our allotment that I have alluded to earlier, was almost exactly a mile and a half's walk away, up on the golf course – I know because my uncle measured it on his bike. I had to go with two empty potato sacks, straight after school, up to the golf course, on as many occasions as was necessary and bring them back filled with dandelions, moss grass and clover and, woe betide me if I tried to bulk out the bags with handfuls of ordinary grass.

This was a kneeling on your hands and knees job all over that golf course and three miles walk there and back to boot. Is it any wonder that I loathed it and I don't know how many of those sacks were ruined, with holes made by them being half carried and half dragged all the way home?

Despite my close involvement with the rabbits and their domain, there were three scenarios during which I was strictly banned from the bottom of the garden, yes banned. The first was, when a buck and a doe were put together, in the same hutch you understand and encouraged to perform the act of mating. Not a sight for innocent eyes, unaware of such mysterious functions of nature but, oh boy, how hard did the imagination work, to try and fathom out this mysterious ritual. The second scenario was when my uncle performed as the dreaded executioner and a rabbit was dispatched from this life, ready for a roast, a pie or a stew. This action was carried out using a two-foot length of tree branch, about the thickness of a chair leg, slightly curved at one end, with a string loop around the other end and which always hung (when not in use) on a nail, on the inside of the greenhouse door. The hapless animal was held up by its ears and dealt a heavy blow across the back of the neck, this being instantly terminal I was assured and all these sordid details I learned in latter days, I hasten to add. The aftermath of the killing, strangely enough, I was always allowed to witness that is the skinning, gutting and cleaning. To begin with, uncle hung the rabbit by a string loop around the back legs, from that same nail on the greenhouse door. Then he would take a razor blade, one of those thick, single sided ones and slice right down the middle of the stomach. I will spare the reader the gory details, but I could be very explicit and describe the whole procedure, having watched a few.

The third scenario was, after the birth of a litter and in the period following, until the young ones were firmly established. This was not so much in the interests of zealous modesty but due to the strange antics of an over anxious mother rabbit, as with any undue or sudden noise or disturbance the litter was killed and sometimes eaten, as well.

So, in these circumstances, I was under strict orders not to venture near the rabbits whilst playing and this was rather powerfully demonstrated as being very necessary, on one occasion. My uncle had arranged, via a newspaper advertisement, for someone to bring his female thoroughbred Belgian Hare, to the house, for it to be mated with uncle's thoroughbred male. This special breed was not for meat eating purposes but for grooming, showing and as pets and they were quite expensive to buy. Yes, yet again, a ban for me whilst the bringing together took place and the intention was, for the resultant litter to be sold off and the proceeds shared. The litter duly arrived some weeks later and I came home from school for my lunch one day, as was normal practice, in the period when the end of garden ban was in force. Because of the potential monetary value of this litter, the ban was even more severely applied, with accompanying threats of consequences most dire.

Whether it was a case of sheer defiance or just uncontrollable curiosity, I shall never know but venture down to the bottom of the garden, I did! How I was not spotted, or how I managed it undiscovered, I cannot remember but I just wanted a sight of those tiny, ginger coloured baby rabbits and I was so careful not to make a noise, or sudden movement, just a peek, that's all. Off I went back to school and returned later, hungry, as usual and looking forward to tea-time, impatient for my uncle to come home at five o'clock, because no meal started until he was home. His inevitable check visit to the bottom of the garden and the discovery of one completely obliterated litter of thoroughbred Belgian Hares was cataclysmic, so much so, that I really cannot remember the shape, form or the extent of those dire consequences that I mentioned earlier! One thing is for sure and that is that no corporal punishment was involved, either on this occasion or at any other time. Well, maybe the odd clip or so round the ear! How strange, though, to be able to remember many quite explicit details of events etc and yet other things seem to be just blotted out? All that I can remember is, that my confession during the inevitable interrogation that I had gone to view, even just a peek at, the precious offspring, brought about an extremely early bedtime that evening and a very depressed household for quite some time afterwards. Anyway, that's enough about those rabbits but just for the record, though, for my friend Jimmy Tyler next door and his parents, it was all about chickens at the bottom of their garden. No room for fairies in wartime days, you will gather!

As I have recorded elsewhere, my mother with my sister, stayed on in London for the rest of the war. I believe that Mum used to leave Lillian with my grandmother, when she went to work, office cleaning and as a waitress in a café. She worked very hard and all her wages, plus my father's service allowance went on providing the best that she could afford, for us two children and this often meant acquiring from the "black market", that secretive, criminal, murky, underworld often making goods available to the general public "under the counter" of bona fide shops and businesses. She would come to stay for weekends, to Upminster, always bringing some normally unobtainable "goodies" like, sweets, blancmange, nylon stockings or extra sugar, butter, cheese and suchlike rationed commodities and even clothing. At this juncture and as another of my asides, vis a vis that patronizing, belittling feeling that I experienced and mention in other episodes, I will tell of some other things that my mother sometimes brought with her.

I had another aunt, Auntie Grace, who worked for the American Red Cross as a teleprinter operator, if you know what that is? She often sent chewing gum and chocolate that she was able to purchase in the PX, the U.S equivalent of our NAAFI for armed forces. However, she once sent two or three blue service blouses, part of her uniform which she wore with a tie, as well, that were hard to distinguish from men's shirts, with the thought that they would be ideal for me for school, thus saving money and clothing coupons. You have no idea how I was ridiculed at school, for wearing girl's blouses and how I felt like inside, when they did so but how did they know? That's easy, really, they spotted the buttoning up on the wrong side and even when I tried wearing the shirts inside out, that did not work, either. I remember being very upset, embarrassed and feeling very inferior and just like the underprivileged class to which I had been likened, because of this sort of treatment.

Back to the subject of food, then. I clearly remember one product that my mother acquired but I received none of it, despite it being in the house over a long period of time and it happened like this. Following some domestic upset resulting in unjust punishment for me, in my view and which I cannot now recall, I remember saying to my uncle that day, in a childish strop, "for that you will get that dreaded disease!" Now, what on earth I had in mind or from where I got the idea, I just do not know but a while later, he was taken seriously ill with diphtheria, no less and my inexplicable prophecy had come to pass. He was seriously ill, as this was a much more life-threatening situation then, than it is nowadays and, of course, highly infectious. I remember being banned again but this time, from my aunt and uncle's bedroom, where he was confined and the white sheet, dipped several times a day in Dettol, hung up right across the doorway – it was just like the sorcerer's lair. Thankfully he recovered but the recuperation process was long and slow, in fact, he was off work for some fifteen to sixteen weeks. Anyway, with a very poor appetite, mainly from the difficulty with eating whilst so ill, even in his recovery process, this was a nightmare for my aunt in those days of rationing. One thing, however, that she always succeeded in getting him to eat was jelly and this is where my mother's "black market" contacts came to the rescue. She got the "unobtainable" and jelly my uncle had, almost every day, all throughout his recovery and his nephew clearly recalls drooling over the bowls of jelly, that he dutifully carried up the stairs on a tray, to help his aunt and to slide the tray under the sheet in the doorway, for uncle to pick up and devour. I also remember scraping out the big dish that the jelly was made up in. What bliss that was!

Finally, an amusing but palatably disastrous story about food. Innovation was high on the priority list of many mothers and housewives in wartime and my aunt was no exception. She was always open to suggestions and new ideas, for making the bland ingredients of wartime diets, more adaptable and tasteful. Now, we always had our meals together, even at lunchtime because my school was only about a quarter of a mile walk away, my uncle popped home for lunch on his bike and my aunt did not go out to work – uncle would not let her. On this particular day, I had finished my main meal before my uncle and so had my aunt. She went ahead and started to serve up "afters" as we called it, except that she did not have any herself, nothing unusual for her. Well, I took one spoonful of the semolina pudding that was served up in my bowl, swallowed it down and my face screwed up as the taste was really terrible! "I don't like this pudding, Auntie" I said, "It tastes horrible" My uncle butted in "What do you mean, it tastes horrible, you've had semolina before, it's on your plate, so eat it" Now, I was brought up under the regime that you stayed seated until you had cleared your plate and wastage was not tolerated. In fact, my father always ruled that what you did not eat at one meal, would be served up for you to finish at the next, so you had better eat it there and then the first time. Somehow, I managed to struggle through this foul-tasting plate of semolina pudding, with even my aunt questioning, why I did not like my "afters" this time? She did not try it for herself, however. Well, now! My uncle took just one mouthful of his dished-up semolina pudding and declared it absolutely awful, quite uneatable, in fact. "Lily, what have you done with this semolina?" he blurted out to my relief, because it was not just me complaining now and the inquest began, with the facts shortly established. My aunt had picked up this new-fangled product called Vanilla Essence in our local Pearks, the grocer's shop and had thought, what a good idea to change the ordinary, over familiar taste of our semolina pudding. The instructions said to squeeze one or two drops to taste, for flavouring purposes, which my aunt, however, did not read. Her thought process went like this: one small bottle, one large bowl of semolina, empty contents of small bottle and that should flavour it nicely. It did not register that the word essence, in the product's name, was not chosen frivolously – it meant very highly concentrated!! Such an innocent mistake even with a barrage of profuse apologies, was scant comfort for the one who had consumed a whole plateful of the vile stuff and, do you know, I cannot recall what affect, if any, the episode had on my internal waste disposal system. Another of those blot outs in my memory, no doubt. That's it, for now anyway, about food!

"THE TIP AND RUN RAID" EPISODE

I have recounted elsewhere about my initial awakenings to matters of an aeronautical nature, the illicit books that came from my father all about aircraft recognition and the profusion of aircraft, daily in the skies overhead. By the time of this very dramatic episode that I shall describe, most probably the summer of 1943, this eight-year-old had become a veritable plane-spotting expert and could even pick out engine sounds of different aircraft, especially the Rolls Royce Merlin, equipping the Spitfires, Hurricanes and Lancasters of the RAF! However, enemy aircraft had always been viewed very high up or only their drone heard, as I have said before, at least until the day that this story took place.

I remember that It was a glorious sunny, morning and we were sitting around the table by the window, in the dining room and overlooking the back garden, eating our breakfast, as was the usual routine. It must have been in the Spring or Summer for it to be so bright at that time of the morning. The time must have been shortly before 8.00 am and later, after the rabbit feeding chores my uncle would set off for work and I would collect the morning paper, before going to school. Suddenly there was the sound of aero engines, which was not an uncommon occurrence with one of the busiest and most vital airfields in Britain, just a minute or so flying time away, R.A.F Hornchurch. "The Spits and Hurries are up early this morning", my uncle said, and I think I just mumbled in reply, because I was listening as the sounds grew louder and I was not sure that they were Spits or Hurries (Spitfires or Hurricanes) because it was not the right engine sound. The loudness of the noise was a little unusual, as well, possibly meaning that the aircraft were unusually low this time and we both started to get up from our seats, to go into the garden to see what was up. I remember saying "They don't sound like Merlin's to me" as we ran into the garden and what we saw, looking up and around takes me twenty times longer to describe or for you to read about, than it took us to witness.

My eyes were first attracted to airplanes over to the left, skimming the rooftops of houses about 100 yards away, on the other side of which was the main London to Southend railway line and they were flying flat out west towards London. This time it was different to what I was used to seeing because they had black crosses and swastikas on them and I shouted out, excitedly, "Nunc, (I always called him that!) they're Jerries', not ours!" Even as I did this, my mind had started to engage in my aircraft recognition mode – German, blunt nosed, single radial engine, low raked back cockpit, mottled camouflage markings and bombs slung underneath, now what plane was it? At the bottom of all the gardens was the line of elm trees that I have described before and as I looked frantically around to see where else the engine noises were coming from, I looked through and beyond the branches of our tree eastwards, as I often did watching the sun come up in the morning, from my bedroom window. There was movement and I shouted out loudly "There's one" By now, my heart was pounding with excitement, but I don't remember fear, just the feeling of wow! Then it burst into my full view directly above us, perhaps some 20 or 30 feet above our tree and, therefore, no more than 200 or so feet away from me - this snarling, roaring airplane! My mind was still racing as there it was in front of me, German, blunt nosed, single radial engine, low raked cockpit, mottled camouflage markings and bombs slung underneath and this time the sight of it, the flash of recall as my mind caught up with my sight and my next shout, were all simultaneous, "It's a Focke-Wulf

One Ninety", I bellowed to my uncle, above the engine noise, in my frantic excitement and pride at my recognition prowess!

The most distinct impression, however, is another of those black and white snapshot pictures that I told you about, at the beginning of all these stories. As I close my eyes even now, over 75 years later, I can still see the head of that pilot, complete with helmet and goggles, looking down out of the right-hand side of the cockpit and straight at this young lad, standing in the back garden, looking up at him – yes, me! Then that unknown German pilot, in his aircraft, flashed over the house and was gone and he could not have been more than about 100 to 150 feet away from me. That's how near I had been to a real, live German airplane and a real, live enemy airman, as well. Thankfully, his bombs stayed hooked up and his guns remained silent for more tasty targets. The railway line to London, the airfield at Hornchurch and some factories and houses had bombs dropped on or near them and the raiders reached as far as Ilford, we heard, before turning back. Soon after, we caught glimpses of them, now slightly higher and being chased by Spitfires, as they returned east toward the coast, the Thames Estuary and back to France. I went to school that day bursting with the exciting, authoritative news and told all who would listen, over and over, all about that Focke-Wulf One Ninety and what it was like to look a German right in the eye!

Incredibly, just recently I was reading Richard C. Smith's history of Hornchurch aerodrome between 1941 and its' closure in 1962. On page 74 he records as follows: 'At 7.30 am on 12th. April 1943, No. 122 Squadron were scrambled to intercept 12 enemy aircraft that had been reported coming in from the north-east at a height of 5'000 ft. When the squadron was airborne and climbing, they saw FW 190's at zero feet, bombing and strafing the Romford and Ilford areas. The interception now became a chase at rooftop height, but the squadron was unable to catch the enemy; although Pilot Officer Edwards and Sergeant Livesey both fired from long range, only Edwards claimed a FW 190 damaged. All the squadron's aircraft landed safely back at Hornchurch at 8.35

am'. I am in little doubt that this was the official record of what I had witnessed for myself – well done little boy's memory!

This is a Focke-Wulf 190 just taking off but in a very similar pose, apart from the half-retracted undercarriage, to the sight that I saw that morning, booming over the tree in our garden. Apart from the pose, this picture only differs in that the upper surfaces are all painted silver instead of the camouflaged colouring that I saw. You can see why the pilot had to look sideways out of the cockpit because his forward, downward vision would have been impeded by the huge engine in front of him. Also, note the 2 bombs slung under the wings, just as I remember it!

The line of houses at the far end of this road are in Howard Road, that ran parallel with the main London railway beyond their rear gardens and over which I first sighted the German aircraft, as I looked to my left on our back doorstep. Our house in this picture is just off the right edge and just showing the corner of the modern-day front garden area, paved over for car parking.

"THE BEAUTY OF A BIKE AND A BRUSH WITH THE LAW!"

One of the amazing things about my childhood experiences, in the wartime, was the remarkable lack of restriction in what I was allowed to do and where I could go, or so it seems to me now, as I think back. In another episode, I shall recall how I was allowed to travel on public transport alone, for instance. I was also free to roam the fields and surrounding countryside at will, with my friends but, of course, I am talking of the periods of light evenings and in the winter only at weekends in daylight hours. In summertime, for example, after eating my tea, I was allowed out to play and with no restriction or bounds other than to be home for bed by 8.00 pm. I remember advocating that an 8.00 pm bedtime for an 8-year-old, should become a 9.00 pm one for a 9-year-old and so on but that made no impression, at all. My point, ignoring this aside is that even in times of war with possible physical harm or danger a constant threat, I had a remarkable amount of freedom to indulge in children's activities. What a difference does the presence of other sinister and more insidious influences, that threaten young people in today's society, make to that situation! So, to that brush with the law. For me, with all this freedom, the real and pressing problem was distance, because the parks, recreation grounds and the fields around in which we played, were all a distance apart and I did not have a bike. Thereon hangs a tale of what can happen when you don't have a bike and yet another, of how you go about getting one of your very own by fair means, not foul!

One of the boys that I thought was a friend, at school, let me regularly have rides on his bike. In fact, it was on his bike that I had sat for the very first time, in the recreation ground that we frequented, pushed off from the bench seat alongside me and completed my first bike ride. As I say, he regularly let me have a ride, especially at lunchtime at school or sometimes after school. Well now, this one lunchtime, with me back early from my lunch at home, I couldn't find this lad, whose name I forget but his bike was there, leaning up against the railings, in the school playground, with all the others. Now came my big mistake – assumption! I assumed that this so-called friend would not mind me having a ride on his bike, just like the many times before. So, I went for the ride down the street, returned in good time for the restart of school and put the bike back alongside the school railings, only it was not in the same place as I had moved it from. That place was taken up by other bikes and I left it some distance further along beside a big tree, maybe 40 or 50 yards away. I went home from school and, later, we were sitting around the table having "tea", as we called it. You know, bread and margarine (not butter with rationing) or maybe crumpets with fish paste, jam, possibly home-made cakes etc. There came a knock at the door and the whole of the local constabulary seemed to be on the doorstep, seeking a lad called Eddie Chambers, who was wanted for <u>stealing</u> a bicycle! I was so terrified that, what with superintendents, inspectors, sergeants and constables, or so it seemed to me, milling about bombarding me with questions, plus my aunt and uncle giving me the third degree, I was in tears! How times change. Could it be envisaged how much interest or involved action that a suspected stolen bicycle would arouse these days and this 'crime' was in wartime, as well. You would have thought that such times would have meant even less to spare for incidentals?

This is Upminster Primary School, my old school today in 2005 with its 70-year-old former pupil leaning on the railings. About another 30 feet or so to the right of this picture's scope is the boundary fence of the school, which runs right down past the buildings and onto the playing field behind. It was at the rear end of this fence that I left the offending bicycle, propped against a tree- so much for being stolen!

Apparently, this so-called friend of mine had gone to get his bike, from where he had left it, to go home after school but it was not there, and the numbskull had not bothered to look any further than the end of his nose for it. He went home, told his parents, they phoned the police and a full-scale search and enquiry was under way, in no time. Check-up calls on this boy's friends unearthed someone who had seen me riding the bike in the lunch break and the call went out to get Eddie Chambers, bike thief. The police wanted to take me into custody, until my uncle persuaded them to test my story first and check the school grounds and, hey presto, the bike was still where I had left it. I still got it in the neck, though, for taking the bike without permission. You can imagine, also, what the school made of it, after all, what could you expect from one of those London East End kids, probably brought up on thieving!

That's the story of when I borrowed a bike, now here's how I got one of my very own and not by 'stealing', either. Following on from the sinful 'bike stealing' crime, a family conference decided that a certain young lad desperately needed a bicycle. The means of this acquisition was quickly determined. This lad (me, that is) would just have to save all his pocket money up, until he had enough to purchase one for himself. You will have noted, that these were not the days of instant fixes to a need, like let's just go and buy him one, right away. I tell you now, that there is no finer way to teach the virtue and to respect the value of, properly acquiring possessions, than to work and save for it. With the assurance of active family co-operation my enthusiasm was aroused and considerably so. I worked for pennies and saved every scrap of money given to me for about a year, before I had enough to pay for a bicycle and the biggest contributor to the fund, was my dear old grandmother, who gave me two shillings and sixpence, pocket money (12½p) each month! This money, plus any other that I could somehow earn or persuade anybody to part with, I took to the Post Office and voraciously purchased Savings Stamps.

The nicest part then was, licking the backs of those stamps and sticking them into this long, oblong shaped book, the evidence of my commitment, on the long, long road to owning my own bicycle. That year long saving saga was exciting, yet frustrating, it was inspiring, yet agonizing but listen to me as I tell you something; it was self-discipline teaching, it was character building, it was value instilling, it was appreciation recognizing and it was downright good for me. Many today would not agree and, no doubt, the benefits of such attributes would not have rested over well with me at the time if I were honest, even if as they probably were, well explained to me. I was too intent on wishing my life away until I had enough Savings Stamps, in enough filled up books to make the purchase, that is, and that part of the story finally happened. Excitement, achievement, pride and deep satisfaction aplenty!

Now, I knew where to go (I had stood outside the shop every day, looking in the window) I knew what model of bicycle that I wanted, what colour, what size, in fact everything about it. I just needed the money represented by those saved up stamps but that was the cue for another, more intense bout of wishing my life away. Well, well, well, little did I think, that the agony of waiting for just one week to go by, could ever outdo the saving up process that had lasted nigh on a whole year, but it could and it did and this is why. You see, filled up books of Savings Stamps were the equivalent of cash, in effect and as such were vulnerable to loss, cashing-in or even stealing, if we were burgled. So, every time a book was filled, my aunt would purchase a National Savings Certificate and I seem to remember that they came in various denominations, although mine were mostly fifteen shilling ones (75p) Once again, these were fixed on to pages in a book and so gave me another but safer one, to handle, fondle, drool over, total up and re-count over and again, most days of the week, I think it was. Then the problem was, that to realize the cash value of Savings Certificates, meant filling in a form to apply for a Post Office Warrant, sending it away and then, waiting for the Warrant to come back – SEVEN WHOLE DAYS LATER! Of course, the time eventually passed but, if it were normally possible to go grey, at the ripe old age of around 8 or 9, then I would have been white at the end of those seven days!

The final great day of waiting dawned, a Saturday; the Warrant arrived, it was cashed at the Post Office and the bicycle shop, Sissley's, was invaded by the Chambers clan. Good old mum came down from London and splashed out on some whizzing extras, like a bright yellow cape, for rainy days, a tool and puncture kit that hung on the back of the saddle and a spanking lighting set, front and rear lamps. We left the shop, everybody else walking home except me. I now had my own transport, a Hercules Roadster Bicycle with 21 inch wheels and from that day on, my body and that bike were welded together, an inseparable entity.   I went everywhere on it; my backside was glued to the saddle, my feet were clamped to the pedals, my hands were bonded to the handlebars. I cleaned it, polished it, would have taken it to bed with me, if allowed, it was my heaven on earth possession and this beauty of a bike was mine, I had bought it, with my money. By the way, over 75 years later, I can still remember the actual cost of that bicycle, without the extras.   It was seven pounds, fourteen shillings and tuppence, £7.14s.2p (£7. 71p) an unbelievable sum and value in today's terms.

DOODLEBUGS (V.1's), ROCKETS (V.2's) AND BUTTERFLIES!

You may well wonder what on earth butterflies have to do with memories of war? This variety was savagely different, though. They didn't flutter, fly or disport a range of beautiful colours, because they were made of metal and they blew up! They were dropped onto densely populated areas by Hitler's bombers, designed and destined for injuring and killing civilians and they achieved that aim. I never encountered a real live one, but I vividly remember being shown a diffused and harmless one at school, which made a very great impression on me. A policeman and someone from the Army, gave us a lecture at our school about them and, although they were much bigger than a real butterfly, this was obviously meant to arouse the curiosity, tempt and cause the finder to touch or pick one up, with very serious or even fatal results, as it exploded in their faces. There was also this big poster, with a picture of one of these Butterfly bombs, pinned on the notice-board, outside the Police Station and for days and weeks afterwards, I looked for these fiendish things, imagining time and again that I had found one, even in our own garden. I recall being frightened, too, more by the threat of these things, than in or of most of my other experiences of war and its many happenings. Quite incredible, really but partly explained, I believe, by the fact that I was getting older by this time, when the Butterfly bombs came down in several parts of the country and the V.1's or Doodlebugs/Buzzbombs and V.2 Rockets were launched onto the civilians of London and other places, in the South of England. I was still naïve and relatively innocent, as were most of my peers of those times but it was inevitable that the realities of wartime and the fears and trepidations of our parents and adult family, transmitted naturally to older children, even though the regime of 'being seen but not heard' was still a reality! That philosophy now defunct, according to today's greater wisdom, was a saving blessing to many of us youngsters of my childhood days, as many will testify. Now look next at the following picture, the first of three that provides visual proof of Hitler's evil intentions.

This is a picture of a real live WW2 Butterfly Bomb. Note the attempted colouring disguise and the "wings". The bomb dropped down as the sides sprung open when picked up and then exploded. A large canister dropped would burst open above ground and spread many of these around and the effect was maiming at best and fatal at worst – kids or adults. Fortunately, their use was minimal.

So, my childlike innocence and naivety were being eroded and my understanding of the dangers of wartime, was probably beginning to make an impact on me. The war had brought a whole load of exciting and adventurous things into my everyday life experience but as I grew older, the realities, outcomes and consequences of war had begun to penetrate my understanding and, sometimes, I was fearful. I missed my mother, too, although my aunt was like a second mother to me and I sometimes found myself wondering whether my father would ever come home again – he was overseas for over 4 years, as it turned out.

I have three main recollections of incidents involving V.1's or Doodlebugs, as they became known as, although I can remember seeing them very frequently passing overhead or some distance away but never very high up. Before I tell you about those incidents, though, some reflections on the phenomena of this, one of Hitler's "vengeance" weapons. Herewith, there was an aura of fear rightly attached to seeing them but, especially, to hearing them, as I will explain, and I remember this, as well, amongst my early realisations of the forebodings of war. No doubt, with these new weapons being subjects of constant daily attention and with me, perhaps, taking more notice of adult talk about them, that fear and dread began to register with me, as well. Firstly, the sight of one and apart from the squat, ugly appearance, the really chilling thing was the stream of fire, belching from the back of the machine, that was so scary and especially so at night. Then, as I said, the sound of them, which had the worst association of fear, full of menace and quite unlike any other airplane sound – you needed not to be an expert, to identify this engine noise. It was, of course, a jet engine (technically speaking a ram jet) and nobody had ever seen or heard anything but propeller engine noises before now. This was very different, a loud but very low pitched, growling sound, almost as if there were a load of objects rattling around inside the engine, not too dissimilar to a very old tractor engine sound. However, the climax of the feelings of menace and associated fear came, when the sound of the engine stopped, because that meant that this pilotless bomb (for that's what it was) was coming down. Sometimes, of course, you heard them and did not see them, like on cloudy days and if the engine noise stopped, you really did experience fear - where was it going to land and explode?

Incidentally, it was widely misunderstood that, the flying bomb was coming down <u>because</u> the engine had stopped, which was incorrect. Conversely, the engine had stopped <u>because </u>the flying bomb was coming down! You see, there was a propeller, a small one in the nose, even on this jet-propelled aircraft and after the pre-set number of revolutions had passed (pre-determined to the estimated distance from launch to the target) the flaps were activated, the plane went into a dive, the remaining fuel that was left in the tanks, slopped away from the pump and the engine starved of fuel, cut out.

This is a V.1.or "Buzzbomb" or "Doodlebug", a pilotless flying bomb with a warhead in the nose. Note the flaming tail, the exhausted burnt fuel, which took on a much more sinister appearance at night, as I relate in one of my stories.

DOODLEBUGS OR V.1'S -A BAPTISM OF FIRE.

My first serious memory of Doodlebugs was the night when I was awakened by one. It was now quite late on in the war, maybe around the latter half of 1944 and we had, for some time, ceased taking the nightly trot into the shelter. The advent of the Doodlebugs, however, reactivated the practice, except for my aunt who had begun to suffer badly from arthritis in her knees. As it happened our neighbours, the Hammonds, on the other side of our house to the Tyler's, had a daughter about the same age as me, whose parents were divorced, and she lived with her father and her elderly grandmother. The father was in the fire service, often on duty and the grandmother was far too immobile to climb down into a shelter and so, it was arranged that us two children would sleep in the shelter together, for safety's sake and to keep each other company.

One night, sometime during the early hours, we were both woken up by this awful, growling engine noise that I have described and both of us shot up in bed, wondering what it was. I quickly clambered out of bed, went to the doorway of the shelter, pulled aside the heavy flap that they had over their door opening and looked out. I was scared stiff when I saw this dark shape of an airplane, clearly, in a bright moonlit sky, flying past very low and with this bright red and orange flame streaming out of the back of it. I called to the girl, "Hey, Edna, look at this airplane, I think it's one of those Doodlebugs" She scrambled to the door just in time to see it, before it disappeared from view and we switched on our torches, looked at each other and we were shaking, most likely with a combination of fear and excitement. A few minutes later, we heard the sound again, further away this time and then footsteps, coming down the path and my uncle stuck his head round the flap of the door. He had hurried round from the ARP Post to check up on my aunt, us kids and the old lady and that was our baptism of fire, so to speak, of

Doodlebugs. The second incident was even more scary and that was during the night as well. This time, we heard the engine sound as if it was right above us, tried to see the thing by looking out of the shelter door again and could not do so – it was a darker night and there must have been lower cloud.

Horror of horrors this time, though, the engine sound stopped and both of us kids just dived back into our beds and pulled the covers up over our heads, although just what real good that would have done us, in the event that the calamity fell on or very near us, I do not know but it sure felt better. It seemed that ages went by and then there was this dull, heavy thud and the ground shook and we were selfishly relieved, because it was obviously some distance away that it had landed. Once again, my uncle and my aunt, this time, came running down to the shelter but my uncle had to leave almost immediately, called away to the scene where the Doodlebug had landed. This was about a half a mile away, in a road called Waldegrave Gardens, just the other side of Upminster railway station. It had fallen on and demolished about 3 houses and blast damaged many others, but I cannot remember any details of the casualties etc. I just remember that real feeling of scariness and panic when that engine stopped.

The final 'close' incident was more amusing, in a way, although dreadful for those upon whom the fiendish thing finally fell, wherever that happened. It was on one of those weekend visits of mine back to London to be with Mum and my sister, that I have referred to elsewhere. I cannot remember what we were doing but Lilian and I were probably playing in the flat and Mum was busying around. Suddenly, I heard the dreaded droning sound of a 'Doodlebug' quite close by. I grabbed my sister, who thought that this was all part of a game, because I dived with her straight under Mum's big double bed, in her bedroom. At the same time, I was shouting out to my mother, "Mum, get down! Get down here under the bed!" "Why, what's the matter", she said. "It's a Doodlebug, can't you hear it?" I called out from under the bed and even my sister had stopped giggling by now. "But it's not stopped, it's going away", Mum called back and then she was laughing. "You look so funny, your legs are sticking out", she said. By this time, the engine sound had died, and I sheepishly emerged from under the bed, as did Lilian. Mum was still laughing, and we joined in, as she said, "If I dived under the bed every time I heard one of those things, I'd never get anything done and you should have seen your legs hanging out!!"

I have wondered since, if this was sheer bravado on her part or an attitude intended to take the fear out of the situation by a wise Mum? Possibly a little of both, I suspect?

ROCKETS OR V 2's – THE UNSEEN AND UNHEARD

Now, as for the V.2 rockets, my memories of or about them, are more to do with my mother's two experiences, which she told us about after each occasion and the impact those experiences had on me, when I contemplated that twice she could, so easily, have been killed and also my sister, in the second of the two incidents. The thing about the V.2 rockets was that, in the vast majority of cases, it was a complete surprise when one struck because they came straight down, with no engine sound and no other means of warning. On the odd occasion, when people just happened to be looking in the right direction and at the right angle, some sightings were reported, of this long cylinder-shaped missile plunging down, in the last one or two hundred feet of its trajectory. I wonder if that was the case at the time of the first of my mother 's experiences? If it was, then the following picture is what would have been seen by the man in the story that follows.

This devilish weapon, a V2 rocket would have been lifted vertically and fired off into the stratosphere, as are modern day rockets and it would have come down, having followed its' pre-set trajectory, to land onto an oblivious target, unseen and unheard until the explosion.

It happened when she was on her way home one morning, from where she worked near Smithfield Meat Market, in London. She was walking along the street, shopping and suddenly a man, a complete stranger, dragged her into a shop doorway, rugby tackle style and shouted at the same time, "Get down, missus" She told us that she was totally bemused and feared the worst, as she fell into a heap in the entrance to the shop. A few seconds later there was this fearful, enormous bang and the ground shook, followed by a lot of noise of breaking glass and thuds of falling masonry and debris, all around her. At first, she was scared to even move but hearing other people moving and shouts and cries, she finally got to her feet and all she could see was clouds of dust, which began to settle on everything and everybody. She looked around her but the man who had manhandled her to safety was nowhere to be seen. This rocket had fallen just by Holborn Viaduct, no more than a couple of hundred yards along the road from where she had been so abruptly and quite unceremoniously dumped into this shop doorway, maybe saving her from blast or flying glass injury, at the very least and no small wonder she was so shaken up. We shall never know, but this may well have been just one of those occasions, when this man was looking in the right direction, at the right angle, at the right time and reacted instinctively. Why else would he have cried out what he did, as well as tackling my mother into the doorway? It certainly made a very deep impression on her and she was convinced that this was none other than God's protection over her, by using a stranger who had saved her from injury or even worse.

The second experience I was a little more affected by but not, happily, by being anywhere near the scene of the happening itself. By this late stage of the war, I was travelling up to London each weekend, to spend the time with Mum and my sister and I will comment on this travel aspect of wartime, elsewhere. After school, on a Friday, was a very exciting time for me, because it was to rush home, have my tea and get off to London to be with Mum but then, of course, I had to face the sadness of leaving, to return on Sunday evening. This was no reflection, at all, on my life with my aunt and uncle but just the natural wrench of leaving my mother and sister behind each time. Anyway, this particular Friday, as I came out of school, there was my aunt waiting for me at the gate, which she never did, and I could tell from the look on her face that this was not going to be good news time. Correct, the news was that I was not going to London that weekend and here's the reason why.

I have related elsewhere, how my mother had moved into another flat, at the top of a block in a street called Goulston Street, one of the main thoroughfares of the more famously known, Petticoat Lane. On this Friday afternoon, which was a main market day in the "Lane", as we knew it , she was at home with my sister now around 4 years old. I am now putting into my own words, from memory, what mum told and described to us, many times over that weekend and the coming days. A V.2 rocket fell at around 12.30 pm in the afternoon, on a large warehouse building in Goulston Street, opposite another building housing the local public baths and indoor swimming pool, only about 150 yards away from our flats and the rows of market stalls and milling shoppers. The explosion was so violent, that mum was convinced that the flats were collapsing, she told us, and she remembers getting up off the floor and grabbing and cuddling my sister. Mercifully, neither of them were injured at all but the shock stunned my mother, my sister was crying, frightened by all the noise and my mother was suddenly concerned about being able to get out of the flat, being on the top floor. All the windows in the flat had caved in, glass, frames, everything and the front door was blown off its hinges. She rushed to see what was happening and through the gaping hole that had been the living room window, overlooking the street below, she saw an appalling sight that she described as being what she would imagine a battlefield would look like. Her next thoughts were to try to go down the stairs to safety and she related how she left my sister with the neighbour in the flat below, to find out more and see what she could do to give help.

Apparently, her battlefield analogy was tragically all too realistic. She said that in the market end of the street, where our flats were, it was chaos with broken glass, debris, collapsed stalls and people milling about dazed, confused and with a lot of them injured and bleeding. As she went up the street towards where the rocket had fallen the devastation was worse. There were dead, dying and injured people lying everywhere, many of them naked or in bathing costumes, blown or staggering from the ruined baths and swimming pool building. She kept dashing back, to the neighbour, to see that my sister was O.K. and then returning, over several hours, helping with distributing hot sweet tea, comforting people and assisting the many doctors, nurses and rescue workers that had converged on the scene. She then managed to get a workman to come up and board up the windows in the flat and fix the front door, to make the flat secure and visited the Post Office, to send a telegram to stop me from going to London that evening. So, that was why my aunt was standing at the school gate to meet me and show me the telegram from mum, which said very little other than that I was not to go to London, that something had happened and that she was coming down, later. Now I understood the worried look on my aunt's face. I joined in with her worry, as did my uncle and we all sweated it out until my mother and sister arrived very late that evening, very tired, very shaken, very dirty but safe. I remembered a similar circumstance involving the late arrival of two people very tired, very shaken, very dirty but safe, some three years before – my Dad and me in Swindon!

For my mother that had been the third time during the war that she had been close to injury or death even, as a result of enemy action and she was only a civilian. Those "Vengeance Weapons" as Hitler called them, were evil instruments of war and it kept us all on edge, as to what else might suddenly descend upon us, even though we were obviously winning the war against Germany and that horribly evil dictator.

THE GOOD OLD "DISTRICT LINE"

In other episodes, I have referred to the astonishing amount of freedom that I enjoyed, to move about and go off and play or whatever, in what were very dangerous and uncertain times. Bearing in mind, too, that attitudes to bringing up children, standards of discipline, behaviour, respect and control, were far more vigorously applied, than in the present liberated (for want of a better description) times and circumstances. Yet, despite this, I was allowed a lot of leeway, at a rather tender age when, in addition to the everyday risks, like being run over or getting lost etc, you could consider the range of other fates that could have befallen me in a time of war. For example, falling bombs, those Doodlebugs and rockets, strafing by" tip and run" raiders (you will remember my story about them flying over the very railway line that I am about to tell you of) and other frightening things and scary circumstances. Well, another of those very surprising freedoms was, for me to be able to go to London each weekend to stay with my mother and sister and travel unaccompanied, at the age of only eight or nine and in such times. This meant a journey on the London Underground, the District Line, which had its eastern terminus at Upminster. As an aside, I can remember reading those adverts, above the windows in the carriages and on posters, repeatedly until I knew them by heart. "Coughs and sneezes spread diseases –

use your handkerchief!" and "Is your journey really necessary?" and "Carters little liver pills" and "Dig for Victory" and "Make do and Mend" and "Mums the word" plus the various long forgotten cigarette brands like Players, Craven'A', Park Drive, Gold Flake and Woodbines etc.

The journey took me over an hour and right into the very heart of London, to Aldgate East (the stop for Petticoat Lane) and right on the boundary of the City of London. Now, many of the trains that I travelled on, were made up of very old rolling stock and did not even have driver-controlled opening and closing doors – you had to grab big handles and pull the doors closed yourself, one on each of the doors, sliding to meet in the middle. Many a time, the train would leave the station, the doors left open by departing passengers (missed by the guard) and would rock along at speed, to the next station and you could stand by the open door, hanging on tightly to a handle or post and watch the tracks and everything else racing by. What a whoosh, too, if a train passed by going in the other direction but nice and cool, mind you, in the summer. Now then, was that dangerous and how about the health and safety aspects of passengers – such things came many years later. As for me, of course, I never did anything silly like standing by the open door, did I?

This is a picture of a District Line train standing in a station on the line to Upminster.
Just by the right shoulder of the second man from the left, can be seen the two central handles that you pulled apart to manually open the doors. The carriage door to the right of the group of women, clearly illustrates its 'unsafe' opening state, being trackside of the train! What a ball 'elf 'n safety would have had in those days!

This picture, although taken many years later, shows the unchanged entrance to Aldgate East Station on the left, as it was during the war. The turning  going left in the centre is Commercial Street, along which I would have gone to go to Gran's. Coming back past the store, on the left, called 'Shopping Centre' for some 100 yards, would bring me to the top of my street, Goulston Street.

BOYS WILL BE BOYS - EVEN IN WAR!

Right at the beginning of this collection of memories, I did say that some of my "flashbacks" would be ordinary, not at all dramatic or spectacular. Here are some that illustrate that the everyday life of this boy was in character with being mischievous, prankish, daring and just like a boy, any boy, most boys in fact and which, not even wartime could smother. For some strange reason, amongst the hundreds of pranks that I must have got up to or other things that I did that were part and parcel of day to day life in my wartime childhood, some certain instances or examples, untitled, stick in my memory.

For instance, in my story about the "tip and run raiders", I talked of the row of houses alongside the main Southend to London railway, over which the raiders flew. At the bottom of the road on which these houses stood, Howard Road, there was a pathway that ran between two of them, enabling people to cross the main railway lines and the London Underground trains terminus and sidings beyond them. The footpath went under a tunnel or arch about 30 yards long, over which the main railway line passed and then over a footbridge, which we called the "Iron Bridge", to cross the sidings. Very often, on summer evenings, quite a number of bats used to fly back and forth through this tunnel or arch and on one occasion, two naughty lads, my mate and myself, took to trying to "down" one of these bats, by swiping at them with long sticks, as they flew along. We succeeded, much to our shame and not only brought one down but killed it in the process and, somewhat in belated mitigation of our crime, we felt very bad at what we had done.

So, we decided to have a ritual ceremony of committal to the bat heaven, if and where there was such a place? We cut up a thickish length of elder bush branch, into about 6 or so pieces, about 8 inches long and tied them together with strips of ivy strand, to make a small platform. Then we laid the dead bat, with wings fully extended, onto this little raft and tied it down with some more ivy strands. With some tender words of regret and best wishes for a happy journey, we launched the funeral raft onto a little stream that ran alongside the footpath- probably a storm or rain drain, because it disappeared into a large pipe when it reached the side of the tunnel. We waved it farewell as it floated serenely into the pipe, the ritual was over, and we felt a little less guilty about it all. Perhaps we had just recently learnt about the Vikings, in school and their custom of launching deceased warriors and kings in burning, funeral longboats, I don't know. I hasten to add that our version was not a pyre and we kept publicity levels of the event very low anyway, just in case of painful reprisals if we spoke of our exploits to anyone. By the way, that word "reprisals" reminds me that as kids in my day we did give heed, without question, to the consequences of our committing misdeeds and that most certainly included some form of what they laughingly call 'corporal punishment' today. We called it getting what you deserved or what you get for doing wrong, in whatever form. This is because that was the way that we had been brought up and to expect and it did work, despite the 'do gooders' claim to the contrary in today's "PC" bewilderingly enlightened society. Their <u>theoretical</u> assessment falters so very badly when faced with the testimony and <u>actual experience of</u> those that lived the code,

<u>not just blather about it or even begin to understand it.</u> Do wrong and there is a price to pay, that's what we knew and expected. Nowadays, reprisal or consequence is deemed barbaric or it's renamed 'counselling' (better described by "come now, sit down here and tell me what's upsetting you") and calls for special needs, schools or specialist treatment or even get away from it all holidays -in Barbados or maybe a skiing trip to Switzerland. Let me record that as a normal healthy boy, youth and young man I was often on the receiving end of my fair share of so called 'corporal punishment' for my misdeeds or wrong doings. My edict on the subject is this. The accumulated physical suffering, abuse or emotional scarring (another 'todayism') that I endured amounted to three main legacies. The first, a few memories of a painfully sore backside: two, a recognition that wrongdoing courted punishment and, lastly, a healthy respect for elders and authority in whatever form. On all three counts as well as many others, in my view, I came out a better self and so did society as a whole. So, what was so different about my circumstances or experiences that leaves me at such odds with current thinking? Well now, the pundits of today's modern methods and academically promoted procedures would probably suggest some psychological, sociological, ecological or a host of other 'ogical' reasons to explain away my wayward philosophy. But why not just accept that many of the traditional, long standing, basic disciplines and ways of life that have served mankind for so many generations may just possibly have it right. Listen to the personal testimonies of those who have lived the code and not to those who hypothesize, project fanciful statistics and advocate change based on flawed assumptions. There is a saying amongst the footballing fraternity that states, "Why change a winning team or formula!" Another popular life attitude says, "If it isn't broke, don't fix it!" Finally, before I get carried away, of course, there were and are those who abuse, take harsh unfair advantage and misdirect the codes of tradition but they are the minority. Instead of changing the rules, the terms of reference, the proven practices and ways of life for the masses, just to

put right the minority element of wrong application, leave alone what works and just deal with the exceptions. The operative word being 'deal' or handle or manage. Just what then is so difficult to comprehend about that? I suspect that a lot of what we are facing here is true about many other areas of life today, in that some real justification must be made for the existence of the expanding breed of academics and university indoctrinated cohorts, of our modern systems of education. How can we advocate the need for all these highly tuned and honed professionals to be launched onto our outdated, crude, unscientific, behind the times and even barbaric codes of life and education, only for them to come back and admit that not a lot needs fixing, really? They would all be out of a job quite soon. So, to set about totally destroying the old, dismantling the proven and the workable and justifying complete change, is their only option. Does all that sound cynical, bitter and twisted, biased and seriously mistaken? By any modern measurement, without a doubt! By my reckoning and by that of a very, very, large band of similarly impressioned people – just sheer, unadulterated, oh so mundane, common sense. But there, I haven't got the problem of justifying my existence or ethos, have I?

This is the tunnel or arch that saw the demise of the bat all those years ago, with one of the culprits holding a minute's silence many years later! The railings were not there in my day and the drain ditch that took 'batty' on his last journey, ran along the left of the path as you view it. The second arch that you can see through 'our' one, was built to replace the Iron Bridge that I mentioned in the tale.

On another occasion, in the same area of our activities, this time across the other side of the Iron Bridge and the Underground train sidings, several of us were exploring the territory, you might say. After a patch of open grassland, there was the boundary fence of the railway property, which also separated between that and the back gardens of another row of houses. At the bottom of all the gardens were the tried and trusted Anderson shelters (just like the one in my Aunt's garden) only, by this time in the war, used much less for protection and much more for uses like storage. We, very naughtily, indulged in a little internal exploration, you might call it, of several of these shelters, otherwise called breaking and entering. Lawn mowers, spades, forks and other equally uninteresting things were not for us but, when we found one with a great stock of tennis balls, that was much more exciting. The problem was that it was at the moment of sharing the spoil that we were spotted by some very irate chaps and did we run. The reason why we ran was, because these chaps were no slouches and were probably some very fit members of the local tennis club, set on catching us culprits. So, not for us the longer path to freedom, of going back to the Iron Bridge to cross the sidings and through the tunnel to traverse the railway line. It was emergency escape route stuff, straight over the tracks, leaping precariously over the live rails of the Underground tracks, up the bank, over the steam railway lines, down the bank and away. When I got home, I had one brand new tennis ball clasped in my hand, which I had found, of course!

Telling this tale of pursuit and escape reminds me of another such a hasty retreat. A couple of us were in an area known as Cranham Chase and on a small hill was a church, less than a couple of miles from home. The best part about this church and the lovely adjoining vicarage, was the vicar's orchard alongside the extensive grounds of this parish seat of worship and just the place for hungry, marauding, scavenging boys on a hot sunny afternoon, to do a bit of scrumping. Once again and why is it often so, at the moment of success and in this case the grabbing of succulent, juicy apples that all hell breaks loose? An extremely irate and put out country vicar appeared on the scene. He must have spotted us up in his trees or perhaps he was just a nosy old busybody? He was nowhere near as agile or fleet of foot, as the tennis club pursuers of another day but, nevertheless, by the time we had reached the ground below our scaled tree, with bulging pockets, he was not too far away and so we flew. Yes, that's right, you've guessed it there was a problem coming up as we ran. There had to be or why else would I remember the occasion so well and thus relate it here? No railway or electrified lines this time to trouble us, just run flat out through the orchard, over the low fencing around the orchard, across the next grassy field and we'd be gone. Trust me to be the victim, too, of the unexpected problem, for as we streaked across this field of quite tall grass, away from the orchard, I ran straight into a hidden section of barbed wire fence and did that wire do its' job. I was tripped by the wire, rolled over several times but jumped up and carried on running. I still have the clear scars of the gouges that the barbs of that vicious wire made, down the calf of my right leg and I spent some time trying to stop the wounds bleeding but to no avail. By the time I got home I had a shoe full of blood, a soaked sock and a whole lot of explaining to do but goodness knows what excuse I made up, not about the wounds but how I had run into barbed wire to get the wounds and I don't remember any pain. I suppose my aunt cleaned me up and bandaged my leg? I just cannot remember, and I put it down to another case of selective forgetfulness – one of those things that the mind blanks out! Many years later I visited the scene of our boyish crime, treading the same churchyard and the same orchard but without climbing the trees. This time, the visit was ended by calmly walking away down the lane!

This is Cranham Church in 2005, changed but little! Over to the left and behind is the orchard still and the fields beyond but I never checked on the barbed wire – though some things never change!

One of our most enjoyable pastimes, was building what we called "camps" and we had several of these, in different places. Some were in big hedgerows around the edge of fields, one was in a small copse of woodland, made from fallen branches, bush foliage, tall grasses and moss and we had a couple, quite high up in trees, as well. Our main one, though, was on the site of two roofless and derelict cottages, destroyed very early in the war, by a jettisoned bomb from a fleeing German aircraft, it seems. These cottages were adjoining, with large front gardens, now overgrown, which made the ruined buildings quite a way back from the passing road and they were less than a quarter mile from our house. Using the plentiful supply of old bricks, pieces of timber and battered doors etc, we made ourselves a cosy hideaway, totally obscured in the dense bushes of the overgrown rear gardens of the cottages. We even had to crawl along several yards of tunnel, made through the bushes, before getting into the den itself. Many a feast was enjoyed in here with scrumped apples, sandwiches from home and suchlike and many an hour was spent, just chatting away in the carefree way of childhood.

In here, too, I distinctly remember making one of the most important discoveries in a young boy's life! One day, my mate Teddy Fuller brought his "girlfriend" to the camp, which was a severe breach of the gang's code of "no girls allowed" There we were just the three of us and well, somewhere along the line, we got around to playing this game called "doctors and nurses", you know, like all kids do? Now, I know what you are thinking, as you read this, but we were only 8 or 9 years old, for goodness sake and, in those days, that age represented pure innocence and sheer curiosity alone. I suspected, on later reflection that this was Teddy's real intention from the off and possible justification for breaking the strict rule about no girls being allowed in our den. Anyway, we make-believe medical practitioners managed to make certain investigatory progress and subsequent discoveries and I definitely profited from this indulgence, because I found out that girls and boys are differently equipped, in a couple of interesting ways, plumbing wise especially and I remember that discovery to this day – how else would I have found out, I often asked myself in later years? By the way, just to prove that we also had other interests to while away time in these dens and I can't remember in which one, but we kept those trophies of war that I have described hoarding, in another story, like the bits of airplanes etc. I can't remember how waterproof these dens were, either or whether we were as keen of them in winter as in summer?

Fishing was another boyish enjoyment and, apart from catching tadpoles, frogs, newts, and sticklebacks etc, there was a proper fishing trip every Wednesday evening, all through the summer. My aunt and uncle were Sunday Bible Class teachers and each week the respective classes, boys and girls older than me in their early teens, came to the house for the evening. The girls did their thing and the boys went off fishing, some two miles away, at a lovely big pond on a friendly farmer's land. As I said, I was by two or three years the younger and, also, the least fortunate, because everybody else had bikes except me, at that time. Sometimes, one of them or my uncle would give me a crossbar lift but, often I would have to walk, which was another of those instances when I felt patronised! On the morning after one fishing evening, I can recall not only feeling belittled but being very angry, as well!

Because of the distance away, I was always sent off home early, too and on this occasion I had been the only one who had caught anything, which were two lovely sized carp. Very much against my will again, I was sent off home with promises firmly established that, my precious catches would be brought back and that I would be able to have them for breakfast, the next morning. For some reason that I cannot remember, perhaps it was later than usual, my aunt gave me my supper and then it was off to bed, before the others got back. The next morning, I was up, early as usual but with the prospect of two smashing fresh water carp for breakfast, the appetite was even keener than usual, although I had no idea what such fish would taste like. So, down the stairs, into the kitchen but no smell of frying and no fish for breakfast. It had been decided, on my behalf and in my absence, to put the fish back into the pond and, boy, was I mad. I remember ranting on that they had no right to do that and they had all broken their promises to bring my fish back home with them. They were just jealous, because they had not caught anything, and I was livid, just absolutely livid with rage. Of course, the right decision had been made and is what was done on all other occasions. I believe that this was a condition of the farmer allowing us to fish, that all catches were returned to the pond. The difference was, that I was only a youngster and had been kidded on, made fun of that I could have the fish for breakfast and been promised that they would bring my catch home. I did not appreciate the big joke at all and my uncle should have told them off for being so cruel, I told myself. All these thoughts went around and around in my head and I was still mad and for a long time afterwards, too!

Speaking of my Aunt and Uncle being Sunday Bible Class teachers, I also went to the same Sunday School. Twice a year there was a big get together, a party at Christmas and an outing in the summer. I distinctly remember looking forward to the 'eats' at the party and the entertainment and games afterwards, topped always by the 'magic lantern' show and the distribution of prizes. The summer outing was always eagerly awaited, with outings to the seaside with all the amusements and fun rides and swimming in the sea. One outing I have extremely painful memories of, however, as we were on our way to Southend-on-Sea on the train. I was standing in the doorway of the railway carriage, which had stopped at a station and along came the guard slamming all the doors left open by departing passengers. My painful problem arose when I neglected to let go of the door pillar that I was holding onto, as the heavy carriage door slammed shut, pinning and crushing my thumb in the process! I spent all that day with swathes of bandages, continually swamped with cold water, as my poor thumb and hand began to take on a strong bluish colour! Strangely enough I do not remember the event causing me to miss out at all on any of the days' activities or maybe my mind just drew a blanket across, erasing all memory, as it often does to unpleasantries.

Many other traditionally accepted boy things were the norm for me, as well, a few examples of which I shall expand upon next. The autumn time was good for endless conker matches and umpteen ideas and experiments for finding ways of perfecting the ultimate, rock hard and un-breakable conker. I can remember that there was no shortage of trees for stocking up with conkers. Another craze occupied me most days, on the way home from school, because you could find me trawling the gutter between roadway and pavement, no, not for "dog-ends" but playing with marbles. You know, bowling them along, taking it in turns, avoiding the drains, trying to hit your opponent's marble, which you kept if you succeeded and then started again, with another marble. This went on until you reached home, and your pockets were either clinking with an excess of these glass balls or you had lost your marbles!

On the main road called St. Mary's Lane, from my school down to our road, Garbutt Road, were to be found lots of local shops on both sides of the road and incidentally, among them was Sissley's the bicycle shop, from which I purchased my bike, as in the story already told. Just before this shop and on the same side of the road, were two vacant premises, still with the wooden fencing across their fronts, not yet taken possession of and still in the hands of estate agents. A broken palisade of the fence of one of these premises allowed us very mischievous lads, easy but unauthorized access. On the wall at the rear of the empty shop was situated a large electrical fuse-box and it so happened that the door of the box swung open quite easily, too. We also discovered that with a piece of wood wide enough, you could touch both of two adjacent metal pieces in the box and you could get this shivery shock run up your arm! I said that we were innocent, did I not? I think we somehow knew that the practice was not recommended but the scientific import of the properties of electric current in exposed terminals, for that's what the two metal pieces were, was not high in our intelligence, shall we say and thus fell into the category of daredevil pranks.

There were lots of other ordinary things that we did, on those lovely, sunny, summer days; like chasing butterflies, burning holes in sheets of paper with a magnifying glass, gleaning in the wheat fields behind the mechanical combine harvester, trying to catch the field mice as they were disturbed and so on and so on. That's right, summer days, because I have very few memories of winter days in my wartime childhood, except being bored in the evenings when it got dark so early. I do remember once when it snowed heavily, and my uncle made me a sledge and I went up and down, with loads of other kids, on the snow covered, sloping sides of a large, partly underground, public air raid shelter in the nearby Odeon Cinema car park, also on St. Mary's Lane. The dark evenings were boring because I had but a very few toys, although books and comics were more plentiful. There were Dandy, Beano, Rover, Champion, Hotspur etc to name a few and board and card games, too, like Snakes and Ladders, Ludo, Monopoly, Draughts, Lexican etc. Another activity featured strongly from about the late autumn, as the evenings lengthened and not altogether to my liking but about which I had little choice. My aunt had me on a programme of making all my own Christmas presents for the family, that's right, making. Believe it or not, she taught me how to knit, crochet, embroider and raffia weave and this young lad became quite an expert in "crafty" matters. He then churned out presents galore, for all and sundry, to everyone's astonished delight, at least, that's what they said, when they received them. Fruit baskets, tablecloths, chairback and arm covers, tea cosies, hot-iron holders, bookmarks etc, etc. Can you try to imagine getting away with such an agenda for girls or boys nowadays? However, this range of skills was not to remain on the agenda of my latter years.

My uncle's sister and brother-in-law lived just up the road from our house and he was an engine driver, like my friend Jimmy Tyler's father next door but on the main-line steam trains that went back and forth between Southend and London, Fenchurch Street. I was always asking him, Uncle Sid was his name, if it was possible to go with him to work and ride on the steam engine or, at least go into the engine shed or sidings, anything just to get onto the footplate. The answer, however, was always in the negative! All was not in vain, though, because my friend's father, our next-door neighbours and the central character in my infamous tale of beery breath and smelly flatulence in the shelter, arranged the impossible, for Jimmy and me to ride on the engine of his train. Probably because his was only a small branch line working train, he fixed it for Jimmy and me to actually ride on the footplate, on the return trip from Upminster to Grays and back, some 20 miles or so. It was only a small steam engine pulling 4 coaches but what the heck, it was a real steam train and we got to shovelling coal, as well. How about that then and in wartime, too. Supposing that 'tip and run' raid had happened on that day?

Another memory that I have of Uncle Sid and Aunt Ethel's house, was that I used to go there each morning before breakfast, to pick up the newspaper for us, as it was delivered with their one. Each day I would come back home, as mentioned before and hold the newspaper up against the kitchen window, for my aunt and uncle to read the front-page headlines of the "Daily Mirror". Some of those headlines I can picture quite clearly, like announcing the victory at El Alamein and the story of the Dambusters raid. There was D-Day of course, but the actual words of the one that stands out so strongly, in my memory simply said, in large capital letters "HITLER DEAD!" To a young lad this seemed to declare that the war was won, everything was now all right, and my Dad would soon be home. At the time of the 60th anniversary of WW2 this same newspaper published reproductions of a significant wartime edition and I was confronted with those same words "HITLER DEAD" the very same newspaper edition of that wartime day, yes, my memory had served me well.

Yet another memory concerned a nasty accident involving Uncle Sid, which I remembered happening, but I did not witness, thank goodness! On the day in question the family were relaxing in their back garden and were all sitting on deck chairs. You know, those wooden frame and canvas contraptions that you could hire on any seaside beach. My uncle was returning, having got up, to sit back in his chair again. Now, most people sat back in those chairs by putting both hands behind them to grasp the wooden side struts of the chair, to take your weight as you lowered yourself into the seat. My uncle did this very thing on this occasion but unknowingly, the struts had come dislodged, probably when he got up firstly and were not properly located in the notches that prevented the whole frame from collapsing. As the frame did just that under the full weight of his lowering body, the two side struts closed together, acting like a giant pair of scissors and trapped several fingers. Fortunately, a neighbour had a car, not exactly common in those days and they rushed him to the hospital, being Oldchurch Hospital, in nearby Hornchurch. His son picked up the severed tops of, I believe, two fingers and held his hands tightly wrapped in a towel in the back of the car but he was quite poorly for several days, having lost a lot of blood during the course of the 25 minute drive to the hospital and one can only imagine what pain he must have been in? I seem to remember that they were not successful, either, in saving the finger tips because the surgery technology was not so capable at that time.

One of my favourite ways of earning pocket money, was to help the United Dairies milkman on his round, on a Saturday morning and it helped greatly during my year of saving up for my bike and there's more about the milk round in another story, later. The milk depot was just some two hundred yards up St. Lawrence Road, opposite our house. It was an early start and, of course, dashing back and forth from the milk cart to the houses, with heavy glass bottles in a hand crate and bringing back the empties the same way, was hard work. There was an added incentive or compensation, though, because this milk cart was horse drawn. If you did a fast, efficient job, you got to jump up on the front seat, before the milkman did, take the reins and trundle the cart along, as we worked our way down the road. Then when we got back to the yard, even more perks were available for the willing, conscientious worker and you got to help to unhitch, walk to the stables, feed and water the horse plus help with the other horses, if you wanted to. The monetary reward, for a whole morning's work was hardly mind blowing, either, about a shilling (10p) I think, which came out of the milkman's own pocket, but I would probably have done it for nothing, just for the horses. Benefits or payment for a boy, in those days, were not always measured in coins or notes, not even when saving up for a bike! So that's a few of those recalled ordinary things that boys do.

These are two pictures of the horse-drawn style milk floats of my day, used by United Dairies, the left one a model and the one on the right a photo of the real thing and just like the one that I rode on.

"MY DAD WAS A SOLDIER IN THE ARMY"

In several of my stories and memory flashbacks, my father has featured in several of them, but I have not mentioned him in any close or intimate way but just as one of those present or of his actual involvement in the event. Perhaps with him being away for so long and from an early age, I got used to him not being in the day-to-day reckoning of my life and probably my uncle partly took his place, not as my father but as the man influence in my life. I knew that I was proud to be able to say that my Dad was a soldier, away in the war but I used to wonder what he was really like as a person and as my Dad. Would I really like him when he came home to live with us again? Would he be stern and grumpy and what things would we be able to do together?

Memories of play with him, for instance, were sketchy, like the time when we played trains, in our flat in Ilford. Surely, he would have lots of stories to tell when he did come home and, at least, I should get my scout knife back, if he kept his promise and I will tell you about that in the next story. I am sure that such an experience was true of many young boys like me, in those times, with fathers snatched away mostly to serve abroad. Perhaps it was different, too, if you were just that little older, when the separation between father and son took place and you would have had more relevant memories to fall back on and nurture? Thankfully, I did not have to get used to a replacement or a so-called uncle, in the father's absence, as so many other kids sadly experienced. What that must have been like and the trauma of the inevitable homecomings of real fathers, I dare not contemplate. What about the fathers that did not make it home at all? What devastation that must have caused to so many kids! Getting back to my own experience, the memories that I have playing or otherwise, of my father prior to the time of war would have been scant anyway, as I was only four and a half when it all began but the ones that I do remember feature in my pre-war reminiscences, which I have recorded, in another clutch of writings. Of course, I vaguely remember his early wartime leave visits home, although I was not always there, when he used to bring me those aircraft recognition books especially and when it was to accompany me, on the several transfer trips from place to place that I have described in other episodes, such as the evacuation trip. I do remember one of his visits, however, much more vividly than most of the others and you will see why, as I describe what happened in my next story. Before that, though, a couple of photos of Dad dressed for and at war.

This first photo on the left is taken when he was on the "Rock", Gibraltar that is and he was in the Royal Artillery, Heavy Ack-Ack, he's in the front row right in the middle, seated. He was responsible for Aircraft Recognition on his gun team and operated the predictor.

I cannot be sure of the location of the photo on the right, although I know that with his contempt for the officer corps, his tongue lost him the stripes. I think it was after he was posted overseas. The shoulder badge depicting an upward pointing bow and arrow, I believe, indicated his operating on anti-aircraft guns.

One day, right at the beginning of my stay in Upminster, I remember being out shopping with my aunt and my mother, pushing the pram with my sister, Lilian, in it and it was certainly before Dad was posted overseas. We passed a shop selling antiques and bric-a-brac etc and outside the shop, on a table, was an array of things and something caught my eye. It was the most terrific looking, black, ebony handled, Scouts knife, in a real leather sheath – a sheath knife that fitted onto your belt. What a great thing to show off hanging on my belt. I could cut twigs off trees, carve pieces of wood, practise knife throwing, and it would be well, you know, mine. I was entranced by it and after a while of hooting, my dear old mum bought it for me and, I believe, it cost two shillings and sixpence (12½p) a lot of money then. Well, now, quite soon after came one of those father visits on a 7-day pass but which actually turned out to be his embarkation leave, prior to going overseas, firstly to Gibraltar. I could not wait to show him my new prize and trophy. That was a big, big mistake on my part. Lots of tears followed, lots of explaining about how dangerous knives were and before very long, that lovely knife was in Dad's permanent possession, for the duration of the war and all the promises to look after it for me and bring it back safely, were of little comfort. Just how much of that action of such mean confiscation, was in the safety interests of his son and how much down to his taking a shine to that knife himself, is open to conjecture, however. Probably to preserve my sanity, I mellowed my extreme disappointment as time went by, to claiming pride in having a Dad that was a soldier in the Army, firing great big guns at the nasty Germans but much more importantly, who was the custodian of my very own, real sheath knife, until he brought it safely home.

It was on one of those visits to London, nearing the end of the war, that I have told of elsewhere, to spend the weekend with Mum and Lilian, my sister, that I recall this next scenario. As usual, I came up the last flights of stairs to our flat, in Goulston Street, calling out "Door!" This was the early warning to open the front door, Chambers fashion. My mother opened the door and I went into the kitchen and received the usual kisses and hugs of greeting. Then mum must have seen the look of curiosity on my face, simultaneous with my spotting this big canvas bag leaning against the wall, with a tin helmet perched on the top. Even more breath-taking was the rifle also propped against the wall. Where did all that stuff come from and why was it there? Then I heard mum's voice (how often have I said that I recall that voice at critical or special times) "There's someone here to see you, son, look behind you" she said. I instinctively turned around to face the door to the front room, to see who else was there and, in the doorway stood this big looking man, in khaki uniform and shiny boots and I said, tentatively, enquiringly, sure but not absolutely sure, "That's Dad" and it was! Father and son together for the first time for over 4 long years and did I have a lot to tell my aunt and uncle and brag about at school, when I got back.

He told me all about the places he had seen and been to, he showed me all his interesting kit and his rifle which was all very exciting but, did he have my sheath knife? Yes, he still had my knife and out it came from the kit bag. I held it, caressed it, I owned it again, for two days but then it stayed with Dad again when I left to go back – oh boy, yet another long wait. I don't really recall everything about that first real father and son reunion, so perhaps the sheath knife took precedence? I think my father was home for 7 days that time in transit, from the frontline in Northern Italy to Austria, where he was to be stationed and billeted, in a little town in the Tirol, called Hermagor, not far from the Brenner Pass, to guard German and Italian prisoners of war. We did not see him for another 6 months or so, until he returned to a camp in England and before his final demobilization into civilian life. That's when I got my lovely knife back, at long last, because he had kept his word and brought it home safely. How this came about, how the new beginnings of post war developed and life thereafter, I shall record later.

"NOW, I'M GONNA TELL YOU A STORY"

I have pinched that line from Max Bygraves because it exactly describes my final tale of reminisce and flashback of my time in Upminster, whilst it was my home. All those things that easily spring to mind of scenes in childhood days that also happened to be the days and times of war and seen through the eyes of this child, me that is. Before I become a raconteur again, though, let me close this chapter of my childhood in a declared, fitting and deservedly appreciative way, appreciative to my dear Aunt and Uncle, I mean. Not that this was to be a final curtain on my activities in Upminster, as you will see as I recount post war and teenage years. I shall touch on the value aspect of my second 'home' again in my memoirs, of that I am sure, because my stay during the war years coincided, for me, with a very impressionable time in any child's life, that between the ages of 5 and 11. Many other children, thrust into the turmoil of war, disturbed by the destruction or split up of home and family and the depositing, by evacuation, into the lives and homes of strangers, were to be differently affected and, all too many, adversely so. For me, after a very short, unhappy experience, in Swindon, of the very thing that I have just described, it was to be a quite different state of affairs. Coincidence or luck? No, I don't think so, in fact, I know so and I'll tell you why. You must identify that I am writing this whole narrative, many years after the events took place, as an adult. I've had time to think this through, analyse things and with greater knowledge, wisdom and informed conviction, I can pinpoint that this was none other than the hand of God in my life. As I have said before, some readers will be clearly sceptical, unbelieving, will nod and mutter comments of doubt, even remark "rubbish!" No matter, as I have already said, my personal, sincere and very real experiences outweigh any doubt or disbelief of others. I can zero into specific and significant time periods or events in my life when God's deliverance or caring influence was or is easily recognized.

The bombing of our home, for example, when I was spared but my dear grandfather was taken and there were to be other definitive events, in later life, too. My stay of almost 5 years, with my Aunt and Uncle, was one of those significant times because it influenced me, my character and the person that I became, to a degree that I am at a loss to quantify – I can speak no more highly of it than that. In fact, I believe that my parents were secretly torn between gratitude and resentment, at this state of affairs. They should not have been because the circumstances that conspired to steer me into and through my relationship with my Aunt and Uncle were not of my parent's inception, for it was just how things were in those times of war and, I say again that it was God's influence in my life. So, to close on this and at the risk of sounding boring, I repeat that I owe so much to Aunt Lily and Uncle Bert and, I know that I told them this in later years, but I doubt that I ever told them enough. As for my parents, well, I only ever wanted to get back home, really, deep down and I was only ever <u>their</u> No.1 son but again, I doubt that I ever told them enough. Maybe, the act of thinking it all through and writing it all down, in my own enlightened words, will amply seal my gratitude and maybe for all of them still, as well?

So, it's back to the story. The scene of this last tale is on one of those Saturday mornings, when I was helping the local United Dairies milkman on his round, for pocket money. On this morning, one of the houses at which I was delivering several pints of milk had two entrance gates to the front garden. The central one that led up to the front door and the other, a bigger, wider gate that ran up to the garage, beside the house. I carried the hand crate with the milk bottles in it, through the smaller gate, put the bottles down on the side of the doorstep and returned but walking across the pebbled front garden to go out of the garage gate. It was as I went through this gateway, with the gate opened back against the hedge, that I saw this bag on the ground, propped up against the base of the hedge. At first, I walked past it, but curiosity got the better of me and I went back and picked up the bag, a black leather one not too unlike my school satchel, except that it did not have a shoulder strap, just a handle and, boy, was it heavy. I took it to the front door of the house, rang the bell and knocked with the big metal knocker, several times but there was no answer. I looked around but there was nobody in the street. What should I do? I decided to take the bag back to the milk cart and tell the milkman about it, he would know what to do.

The milkman and the other boy helping that morning, were a long way down the road delivering, so I hung the bag on the hook next to the one on which the horses feeding bag hung and carried on with my list of pints to deliver. I then just forgot all about that bag, probably because I was concentrating on trying to finish my calls, so that I could jump up and take the reins, to get "horsey" to trundle to the next stopping point, before the milkman came back to do it himself, which I successfully did. So, we carried on until we finished the round, dropped the other lad off at his home and went back to the yard and, while the milkman went into the office to do his books, I went to do my usual enjoyable, quite voluntary chore, of helping with the stabling and feeding of the horse. With that pleasure finished, I went back to get my "wages" from the milkman in the office, but the office was locked, and the milkman gone, home probably, I thought. What about my wages, though? Oh well, I decided, I would just have to wait until tomorrow and try and catch him on his round. I went back through the yard for a last pat of "horsey's" nose, walked past the parked, unhitched milk cart and looked straight at that black bag, hanging on the hook where I had left it – I had forgotten every bit about it. I hopped up onto the cart, grabbed the bag and shot out of the empty yard, with a real sigh of relief that nobody had seen me.

But what was I to do now? There was nobody to give the bag to in the depot, the stable man had nothing to do with the milk rounds, because he only looked after the horses. There was nothing for it but to take it home and try to explain, to my aunt and uncle what had happened. However, the closer I got to home, the heavier the bag got and the more that I began to worry, about what my aunt would say and, more frighteningly, what would my uncle say when he came home? They would both tell me off, for not having told the milkman straightaway after I had found it or that I had not handed the bag over, as soon as we got back to the depot or why I had not gone back to the house even, outside which I had found it? I had thought of that last one but decided that, the people might not believe me or may accuse me of stealing it. I had found the bag in the morning and it was now late afternoon so, whatever way I looked at it, I was sure that I was in for it. By the time I reached home I was decided on my next course of action. I would hide the bag, in the bike shed. Then, I would take it into the depot the next morning, when my friendly milkman would be there, who I felt would understand my serious predicament better, would know what best to do and I could get my wages, at the same time, couldn't I?

It was not to be as simple as that, though and matters got decidedly trickier, in fact and all down to curiosity. Because of going to church on Sunday mornings, I was unable to sneak off to the milk depot to catch the milkman and the depot was closed by midday, too early for me to go there after church. That was bad enough, but worse, much worse, all through the service as I weighed up what to do, I began to wonder what was in that bag? I succumbed to the dreaded temptation to see what was so heavy and I also thought, to justify myself, perhaps I could get a name, address or some clue as to the owner. So, after church, out in the shed behind the bikes, I grabbed the bag, clicked up the catches, opened the flap and looked inside. My eyes must have popped open wide and I must have gulped for air, because I absolutely shook with fright and excitement. This bag was full of money! I had never seen such an amount of money in one place, in all my life. There were bundles of notes and bags of coins and a lot of loose money in a large inside pocket – no wonder that bag was so heavy. Now what? Nothing else for it, I just had to tell my aunt and uncle all about it, because this was now very, very serious and I was in one big heap of trouble already, without so much money being involved, as well. So, after agonizing over it, I plucked up the courage, went indoors and blurted it out. They were almost speechless, and my uncle rushed out to the shed, to retrieve the bag and took it indoors to verify what I had told them and, as I expected, the big cross-examination began, and the lecturing went on and on and on.

First thing on Monday morning, I was marched up to the United Dairies depot by my uncle, into the Depot Manager's office and I was made to relate the whole story. My heart sank to the floor when the Manager said that the Police would have to be informed of this, the bag handed over to them and the stern look on his face scared the wits out of me. But, in the meantime, I would have to go to school and we would be contacted later. That day, at school, was a very, very long and miserable one and even more so, when I went home for lunch, as usual and nothing had been heard, either from the Depot Manager of the dairy or the Police. However, when I got home after school later that day, the dreaded contact had been made and my uncle and myself were to be interviewed next morning, at the local Police station. What was to be the outcome, I wondered, with no little degree of fear and trepidation. Would it be the same policemen who had nearly marched me off from home over the "stolen bike" episode? If so, then I was in for it!

In the Inspector's office of the Police station the next morning were my uncle, me, the local Police Inspector, the dairy Depot Manager and another man that I did not know. We soon found out who he was, though, none other than the owner of the lost black bag. As it turned out, he had been traced by information gleaned from papers found in the bag, together with the money. He was the manager of a firm of rent collectors that collected rents for all the local estate agents. It was explained to my uncle and me that, on the morning when his bag went missing, he had called on the house where I delivered the milk, driving his little car onto the side pathway to park in front of the garage. When he came out of the house, having done his business, he put the bag down

137

by the hedge to open the gate, got straight in to reverse into the road and drove off to a meeting, forgetting all about the bag. On discovering the loss, quite a while later, he remembered what he had done, frantically returned to retrieve the bag but, of course, I had come along in the meantime and the rest was history. There was nobody at the house either, as I had found out when I picked up the bag and knocked. They must have gone out soon after doing their business with the rent collector. He had reported it all to the Police, of course and then, when the dairy Depot Manager had rang the Police on the Monday morning, as he had said he would, all the pieces had fallen into place and now everything was explained in this meeting and much to the relief of all concerned that it had all turned out so well.

I doubt if there was anyone more relieved than me and I began to just believe that I might get away with things a bit lighter than I feared earlier. However, I was totally taken aback as things then happened that were such an excitement to me that I nearly cried with happiness. Firstly, the Police Inspector exonerated me from any blame or wrongdoing other than being a bit careless and that was great. Then, the relieved Rent Collector, who had got his bag back, was most complimentary about my honesty and diligence, in looking after the bag when I had found it and that was great, too. But then his next action was the thing that really got me panting because, he insisted that with my uncle's permission, I should be suitably financially rewarded, and he proceeded to take from a wallet, a great big bundle of notes. Then, would you believe it, he started to count out £1 notes, laying them down on the desk in front of him. One, two, three he counted, and he went on ten, eleven, twelve, thirteen, then eighteen, nineteen twenty and by now my heart was pounding. Was he really going to give me some money for looking after his bag? Was it really going to be all that he was counting out on the table? Still he went on

counting: twenty-seven, twenty-eight, twenty-nine. I thought to myself, I would be able to go and buy a brand new and better bike than the one I had, right now. He got to thirty, yes, thirty £1-pound notes, in a pile, there on the desk in front of all of us. He looked up at me, at my uncle and then at the others in the room. Was he really going to give me all that money? He picked up the bundle of notes and then...... I woke up! Sorry, folks but it was all a long, long dream! How cruel are dreams, eh? But what a dream to have and what a story it makes to pass on – a real shaggy dog one, as they say. It was so real at the time, though and as I lay in bed after waking up, going back over it in my mind, you can imagine the disappointment that came over me as reality set in. I have never forgotten it and the telling of the story of my dream has often caused more than a modicum of consternation, shall we say!

Well now, there are many, many more memories that linger because, for a very long time after war was finally over with the fall of Japan (VJ Day) following on from victory in Europe (VE Day) the basic atmosphere, the routine, the lifestyle, most of the restrictions, including rationing and the very "feel" of those wartime days hung on. Despite the relief and joy of winning; the fact that freedom was in the air again, the lifting of some of the restrictions like no more miserable "blackout" and the sheer pleasure of no more worry about bombs, planes, V1's, V2's, sirens and all that stuff, the after effects, the smell and the hangover of war could easily be revived in the mind and the senses. Rationing of food, clothes, sweets etc continued. Shortages of and absence, too, of many things taken for granted in peacetime would take a long, long time to end or return. Who could miss all those bomb-sites and the many damaged houses and buildings, for instance? Then there were the Air Raid Shelter signs, the sand bags, the taped glass windows, the hoardings instead of shop fronts and still lots of uniformed people everywhere, still many Mums and Dads away from home etc, etc, etc. Many months and, indeed, years would pass before it was all changed over to peacetime imagery and all these many other memories, I hope to record in ensuing ramblings but for now, with this lad coming up to 10½ years old, life's experiences were going to change again. There were still a few more years of child's eye 'viewing' ahead but wartime would give way to peacetime, childhood would creep into teenager time and growing up would bring a whole host of new and different challenges and experiences, in a much-changed world, for me to recall and record years later.

A FINAL THOUGHT

I lived and saw these experiences "through the eyes of a child" but wrote them down much later in the style and language of an adult. Let me just take the reader back to the episode entitled, "The stuff falling on my back" where I have recorded that the events so described, took place on the night of the 21st.October 1940. I have just completed this first writing down of these my family beginnings, my earliest recollections and my childhood memories, mostly in wartime. In 3 days' time, it will be 64 years ago that that 'stuff' fell on my back, my mother's voice called out my name and my Grandad went out of my everyday experience. I do not apologise for repeating that with all these events amazingly, almost unbelievably in my memory, the realism, the clarity and the sounds even, are all just like it took place only yesterday! I expect that it will always be so and, therefore, will always be a constant reminder of the difference, to me, of having God in my life. I believe that I have a much deeper appreciation of what, I feel, that I owe to God's incredible blessing, care and protection over all the years and through all the experiences of my life. That conviction is a deep one, remains with me to this day and always will.

Eddie Chambers – 18th.October, 2004

ALL TOGETHER NOW

"HOME AGAIN AND POST-WAR STRUGGLES"

Before I launch into the next phase of my memories, my story would be deficient for the exclusion of my two smashing sisters. Also before I continue my storytelling, let me just record what present day looks like, as opposed to the historic point reached in my storytelling, with a picture of all three of us as adults, taken in 1984. Lillian, in the middle, is the one that arrived just before Dad went to war – his going away present! We went through the war together, not always physically so but as an experience, without doubt. Ruth arrived within 10 months of Dad coming home from the war – his coming home present! I love my two sisters in different ways and for different reasons and we have had little or no occasion to fight over the years.

THE TRIO

Sadly, Ruth and I lost our sister, Lillian, to breast cancer in June 1999, only 59 years of age and Ruth and I missed her greatly then and the pain lingers on still! Strangely, for me anyway, the loss was harder, too, than even the loss of my parents was – my Mum in May 1987 and my Dad in April 1992. Many say that the loss of siblings is often more significant and being the eldest I can vouch for that, because I've had it three times over in my lifetime, losing 2 brothers and a sister – John, David and then Lillian!

So, following on from where I left off, there is now a trio as grownups, with families of their own and this provides the major reason for me wanting to leave an insight into my and our history, for the children, grandchildren, great grandchildren and so on, who will follow.

ALL TOGETHER AND HOME AGAIN TO POST WAR STRUGGLES

After the end of my first collection of memories, I've thought a lot about things since writing them, friends and family members have read through my first 'offering', for the want of a better description and from both camps I am encouraged to continue, so here goes with more memories.

No special titles top the page, as I launch into the period of my life that would see the real me beginning to take shape as a person; learning the lessons according to my surroundings, my circumstances and the family's resources and traversing the various phases that influenced how my life developed. I have a reason for no titles, but it only occurred to me, when I actually tackled the question of what I should call the next writings of my memories. I decided that I didn't really need to call it anything or give it a 'special' title. You see, the word special is often misused, as most words are at some time by someone, somewhere, I suppose. What I mean is that the word 'unique' is a more appropriate one to use to introduce the next phase of my memories, because that means that what I intend to write and what I will record is not special, except to me but it is unique. We all are unique, in fact, we are never exactly reproduced and therefore, somewhat confusingly from this one aspect alone, we are equal. So, no special titles, just more of the same as I 'label' each memory or flashback. What you will read about are ordinary things, as well, everyday things and many of them will not have anywhere near the same degree of uniqueness as others will have. No matter, I have never yet come across a totally interest lacking, uninspiring or lifeless story of another person's experiences, as I have learnt about them, read about them or listened to them recounted. There is something just different, as I say and captivating about everyone's story, if not in the telling, then in the effect and the outcome on lives, events and how things take shape. All of this philosophy stuff has very little to do with what I need to get down to, in the recording of my memories but at my age now, I think that I can indulge from time to time, without too much recrimination. So where shall I begin, again? From right where I left off, I suppose, will be best but no, not with another dream story! First though, I will make several opening observations...

To begin with, speaking of titles again, "East of the City of London" is what is titled on the front cover and the first inside page of this whole collection of writings. You may well have asked or queried silently, what was so significant about Aldgate Pump, to which I will add some explanation. Apart from any historical or geographical reason, it was a point of reference or symbol to me, of the separation of the business world or 'inner sanctum' of the City of London and all its connotations of power and wealth and the real world of ordinary people that I was part of. It was also the point where asphalt pavements started? Your next unuttered question might be "asphalt pavements, what's all that about?" Again, all will be revealed later, on that one! My next observation about Aldgate Pump is that I was born barely 3 miles from the "Pump" and that the word 'beyond' in the book title, as far as my home was concerned was not to really apply to me for many years to come. It was now late 1945 and I would live within 1 mile of Aldgate Pump for the next 27 years, within 2 miles for the following 8 years and still within only 3½ miles for another 21 years after that, before finally 'beyonding' to Kent, to invent a word for my purpose. However, unlike many of those of yesteryear, who lived and breathed their whole lifetime within a small radius of their birthplace I would be privileged in later life, like an increasing number of people, to visit and stay in many places throughout my own country, all over Europe and all around the world. To have predicted such to me, in the days about which I presently write would have been met with total disbelief, in fact "not a hope" would have been my response. To get back to my narrative, though, after 6 years of war largely in the nearer 'beyond' of Upminster that is, I am now in my real family home in the 'East of the City' of the title, in the world famous 'Petticoat Lane', with my mother and my sister and soon to be, with my father, too. Not long after that with another sister but that is jumping the gun, as they say.

The final observation is that the material and impulse for what I write down, is the same as for all my earlier writings – those flash backs of events and happenings or snapshots in your memory, if you like. No diary record this, because what I write I cannot consistently get into being chronologically correct and I don't believe that that really matters, either (I have said before, though, that it does improve as I get older) Perhaps it's better for the reader that way, too, there will be no need to get used to a different approach – so there you go. Remember, that an overriding premise, as well, is not only to record the events themselves but to try to convey to the reader the atmosphere and the ambience of the times surrounding those events. So, then, I will now pick up the story again.

You may remember that before telling you about my dream at the end of the first story collection, I told you about my lovely scout knife still in my fathers' possession? Well, as I returned home to London to live, the prospect of that knife also returning home when my father got to come back, began to take up a lot of my conscious thinking. However, let me air some thoughts about leaving one 'home' to return to, what you might call, my real home. You will recall that I have recorded that a lot of my early and childhood life and memories very much involved the 'home' at Upminster, that of my Aunt and Uncle. I had now completed some almost five long and continuous years in that 'home' and it was very much that to me, as well. I would greatly miss my Aunt's love, care and influence and although I did not realise it so much then, I would miss the austere, sometimes stern influence of my Uncle, too. I have written it down before and I have no hesitation in doing it again, as I record that I owe an awful lot to who I am and what I am today, to the way that I was taught and brought up whilst living with Auntie Lily and Uncle Bert. It was there that I became a Christian and such principles were often rigidly practised, much to the disapproval of many and amongst my readers, too, no doubt. I can only record that I know what I am stating, it's not just an opinion or an attitude but a vital, proven, lived out reality to me. I hasten to add that the 'Bible' way of life was practised by my parents and throughout my family but with varying degrees of rigidity and application. I think that this will reveal itself as my story embraces living standards, individual lifestyles and the working out of their beliefs in their own daily lives. In other words, what it really is and means and how it works out for each individual to be a Christian. I suppose that the one thing that a change of home does confirm very forcibly, though, is the bond between a mother, her children and between siblings and explains why I always wanted to visit London, whilst I was away and why I still was able to break with Upminster to be with Mum again, when it was time to do so. Who knows, though, recalling what I wrote about those rather demeaning attitudes that I sometimes sensed in 'snooty', superior, rural Upminster, I may even have been more at home, you might say, back in London? There was yet another very good reason, though, for being pleased with my changed environment and something joyously important in any child's reckoning. I was back near my Grandma again. Yes, that's right that Grandma, the other half of the Grandad that I had lost, and she was still living in that same flat, still the Caretaker of College Buildings. Just as with my mother and sister, I had been restricted to infrequent visits, in my relationship with my grandmother for nearly 5 years. There would now be many a visit to her home and

many a special snack prepared to take to school, because I had
to go past Gran's place to go to school every morning. I could
see that there were going to be lots of compensations to
coming back to London, despite the other changes. There was
the other Grandma, too, Dad's mum but as I mentioned
before, I never really got as close to her.

BACK IN TOWN!

Things were certainly different! To begin with there was no
garden, no sprawling, roaming fields with all the adventures
and the fun and the open spaces and fresh air. A very much
smaller home in size, too, just 3 small rooms and an outside
toilet on a back balcony. What's more, it was sat at the top of
our block in the flats, in Goulston Street, looking down on
one of the main thoroughfares of the famous Petticoat Lane.
You may remember that my mother had moved to here,
following the bombing and the return from Swindon, back in
late 1941 or around that time. To illustrate for the reader there
follows some latter-day photos of our old flats. The top was at
the end of nine flights of stairs, too, all 69 steps of them but
that was no sweat to my young, strong and agile legs and
body. Coming down them was another thing altogether,
though and I can remember the pattern of thumps as I
descended, as clear as can be. It went like this as I bounded
down two steps at a time. Bang, bang, bang and thump as I hit
the landing floor, then pat, pat two steps to the right across the
landing and bang, bang, bang and thump, as I hit the next
landing and so on eight times over until the ninth time, when
there was only one thump because with only 5 steps, I cleared
that in one bound! In no time at all I was on the street. Going
up was a bit of a drag for Mum, mind you but us kids took it
in our stride, as I was now going on 11, Lillian was still baby
sister about 5½ years old and she soon became my shadow, as
you will see. All of us used our call out system for getting the
front door opened as we climbed the stairs well in advance of
reaching it. You started to call out, in a loud voice, "Door",

when within 2 landings of the top and whoever was in the flat obligingly opened the front door and that was very welcome after 9 flights of stairs with hands and arms loaded with shopping.

The following pictures are of our flats in Petticoat Lane when they had been emptied and allowed to go derelict, prior to being purchased and totally refurbished into luxury apartments. The left picture is the front view and our old front room window is at the top to the right of the central stairwell with the railings in the apertures. The right picture is the back view with Mum and Dad's old bedroom window, again at the top to the left of the central back balconies. On these balconies were the outside loos, the coal cupboards and the door into the kitchen. Dad enclosed our one at the top with glass-still evident. The windowless aperture at the very top was the communal washhouse and drying room on the roof, the same roof as in snowball stories that follow later! The yard of other flats in the foreground is functioning in the same way as in our day – the football and cricket pitch!

As I say, the play facilities and the space were all so different to the country, as we called it. However, youth and tons of energetic exuberance are the breeding ground of invention and adaptation and sheer making do. Hitler's evil and devastating handiwork over the war years had left lots of previously unavailable play areas, called 'bomb sites' and we became experts in gaining access to and fully exploiting such a paradise of opportunity.

This was especially true of many sites, long fenced off and now positively sprouting with growth, vegetation, new shrubs, wild flowers etc, some 4 or 5 years hence from the original bomb damage and we had names for them all. There was Burma Road, Moorgate, City Park, Cinders and so on, all potentially dangerous and officially out of bounds. What the heck, that only added to the fun. Many a time we were chased off or almost caught by the "cops" or site watchmen, but we knew all the escape routes, the back ways and how to just disappear. We had camps built in dozens of places, with no shortage of raw materials, bricks galore, timber and boards aplenty and no problem with labour. When I think back now to our clambering all over derelict, ruined skeletons of buildings; climbing those staircases that had few treads left, balancing across floor joists that had lost all floorboards and sometimes 2, 3 or more floors up, or probing around dark, empty basements and so on, I shudder to think what might have happened?

The real fun, though, was on those sites that had been cleared and levelled down to the foundations, sealed with tar to stop leakage and brick wall surrounded, to serve as water storage tanks or reservoirs for firefighting purposes. They always had large white letters painted on the walls EWS, which stood for Emergency Water Supply or some such thing. Sometimes these were as large as football pitches, as once they were very large buildings and just right for raft building and sailing about, even only on long thick planks and just punting along to your hearts' content. Yes, we could have drowned, too! If any reader gets the chance to see one of those old Ealing Studios classics called "Passport to Pimlico", you will see portrayed something of what I am describing, played out in that film. The group of kids portrayed in that film could so easily have been myself and my band of mates. The hierarchy of membership, having so-called 'leaders'; the whole business of there being gangs with special names and territories in which they separately operated, boundaries over which you crossed with great care etc, was so like what I am recording as part of my stories. I cannot fault the portrayal of what it was really like and not only in London, either but in other towns and cities, too. So, you see, it did not take long to replace all the potential for fun and play that I had enjoyed, in 'the country' and I'll relate more of that sort of stuff after the following picture. It is a fact that changes in circumstances do not always result in a spoiling of playtime and having fun. The ability of kids to adjust and innovate is well accepted and that is what we had to do, because if we didn't there was no recourse to anything else. No expensive high-tech toys or activities as alternatives. The best way that I can demonstrate what I mean is with the help of the following picture.

This picture, on the corner of Whitechapel High Street and Osborn Street, shows a whole series of buildings swept away by bombing, the standard low brick wall surrounding the site and the empty

space on the other side down to the foundations – a typical bomb-site and a paradise for roaming, building ramshackle camps and whatever.

Talking of water, always a medium for fun for kids, the nearest source of water on a grand scale, of course, was the

River Thames and did we soon get to know that well and especially down by the greatest, most unique river bridge on this planet bar none, Tower Bridge! Through the maze of alleys and streets on our scooters we could be down by the river and the beach in under 15 minutes. The beach, you say? Yes, the Cockney's seaside, that 150 yards or so of sandy beach with stone steps down onto it and complete with deck chairs, just like Southend ("Soufend") or Ramsgate ("Ramsgit") or Herne bay ("Ern Bay") to pronounce in the vernacular, but without the fun fairs.

Being tidal, the river made it even more like the real seaside and this 'strip' was on the north side of the river, on the upstream side of Tower Bridge, between the bridge and Tower Pier. The Pier was significant, too, where the paddle steamers (the 'Royal Eagle and 'Crested Eagle') started out their day-trips, that's right, to "Soufend" etc and having to get the bridge raised to pass through, both outbound in the morning and returning in the evening. We used the Pier for other things, you see, like diving off the supporting pillars into the river and I can still vividly remember the murky, yellowy water as I opened my eyes when submerged. Of course, we were always being chased off the pier by the Police or the Port of London Authority (PLA) staff, who controlled the Pier.

Like all youngsters, we were blind to the dangers of boats and the currents but I'm glad to say that we never had or heard of any accidents. We used to roam all along the streets serving the old riverside wharves, as well (those still left standing from the Blitz) but docks security was pretty good, as were the Thames Police in their launches and we only really managed to get down to the waterside via the public stairs – stone, wide and slippery, although sometimes we made it onto the barges moored alongside the wharves. I can remember, too, getting into the derelict acres of demolished buildings surrounding the inner locks, such as what is now luxuriously redeveloped like St. Katherine's Dock etc. We constructed our own rafts and then sailed the deep waters of those locks. Now that was dangerous in the extreme, but I and we survived. So, you see we had our own ways, means and varieties of water sports, us Big City kids and just in case my readers suspect a little exaggeration or a fantasy memory, I've found the photographic evidence to support my every word – well, nearly every word.

The picture on the left illustrates the diving into the river, although we used to climb onto the support timbers under the wooden pier in the picture. Who knows that may even be me diving in! Note the

cranes in the background. The picture on the right clearly shows those steps that gave access right down and into the river. The shadows tell it to be a warm sunny day and the absence of swimming trunks was no put-off.

A NEW SCHOOL

I suppose that the first real challenge about coming home was going to a new school. Getting used to different living quarters and lifestyle was no problem, because I was with Mum and a playmate, my sister, even though much younger, which was something that I had not had in Upminster. I was the boss, too and Lillian loved having a big brother to follow around and copy, as much as I enjoyed having someone to

152

share with. My new school was Christ Church Primary, in Brick Lane, attached to Christ Church, Spitalfields and only some 10 minutes' walk from home. I was to go through to take my 'eleven plus' at that school, waltz through with ease and qualify to go to Raine's Foundation Grammar School for Boys, as it was augustly titled. Lillian also followed me on that route, to the girl's school though – I told you that she was my shadow. I remember clearly, sitting that eleven plus exam and finishing the paper with oodles of time to spare, much to the pride of my teacher, Miss Kendrick, whose favourite I clearly was. I readily confess, here and now, to having had a serious crush on that lady and I could have married her without a second thought, were it not for the slight difference in years. She allowed me out of the room early, that exam day to go and play whilst the others finished out the time, which is all that I had to relish for my efforts to please and impress her, sadly. Surely, I deserved a little peck on the cheek. I left that school never to see her again and I have absolutely no idea how she managed thereafter or got over it – losing me, I mean?

Behind and beside Christchurch school playground was a park, also part of the Church grounds, which rejoiced under the name of "Itchy Park!" and there were 2 reasons for the name, it seems. Primarily, the trees that grew there shed seed pods that were easily burst, deposited down your back, releasing a very irritating sort of powder, which resulted in extreme fits of scratching – were they sycamore? Secondly, as the years went by the park became the haunt of meths (methylated spirits) drinkers or 'winoes' as they were called and they were mostly, poor, unkept, unwashed and just so very 'itchy' Conversely, there were separate and fenced off swings and a play area for the younger children and the school playground itself which, quite strangely, never seemed to conflict with the close proximity of undesirable characters or have the same evil connotations that it would have had today. What has changed in our world and how have we allowed the evil doings of mankind to gain the upper hand in so many ways?

This is my first school back in London, Christchurch Primary/Junior in Brick Lane, drinking water fountain and all.

LIFE'S NEW DAILY ROUTINES

Life began to take on a pattern, suited to my new surroundings and I began to fulfil a role, too, for my mother that I both took to, enjoyed, developed and which began to form part of the character that I was to become as a whole person, which I recognised years later. It was something that gave me immense pleasure and must have been a real blessing to my mother who began to lean very much towards her number one son. It was simply that I just could not do enough for her and pleasing her by doing more than she asked me to do, was especially pleasing for me, too. I used to rack my brain to think of ways and means to surprise her by doing the unexpected. Now, don't get me wrong, I was no saintly child and I used to moan like heck at some of the chores that I had to take on. I did them but because I didn't like them, I felt entitled to moan about it, as well. As I say, what gave me the most pleasure was doing the things that I hadn't been asked to do, chores and jobs done and dusted that took Mum by surprise and that she wasn't expecting to be done or not done so quickly. I sometimes used to mess up and not make too good a job of it, but Mum would then show me the way that it should be done and we both profited by that. Of course, most of the things that I am talking about were to do with the upkeeping and cleaning of the flat and running the errands.

But my mother had been a waitress (a Lyons Corner House 'nippy', no less) and an Office Cleaner, for all her working life and she had 'degrees' in her professions. So, all the finer points of floor cleaning, sweeping, scrubbing, oven cleaning, ironing, paintwork washing, carpet beating, dusting, window cleaning and so on, I learned from the expert, my Mum! Each morning Mum would be gone to work just before 5.00am to do her office cleaning and be home with barely enough time to get us breakfasted and off to school. This is where I learnt to help, by getting myself up on time, getting washed and dressed and then making sure that Lillian was seen to, in the same way. I shall never forget the exasperation of doing up those endless buttons on her liberty bodice – they drove me to distraction! Each morning I would race to try and get that much further ahead than yesterday, before Mum got home – that bit more that she wasn't expecting to be done. Each evening, as we got home from school, just after 4.00pm Mum would leave for her second office cleaning job, a different venue and I held the fort until she got home to cook the evening meal. It was always more of the same for me, peel the spuds or prick the sausages or just have everything out ready for her to make a start, just anything to try to improve on what I had achieved on the last evening.

When Friday came it was even more of the same sort of thing, but I always had a special job for Friday evening and that was to clean the cooker. You know, one of those blue check and white New World Gas cookers, with 4 hobs, an under grill, the oven and all its' shelves and the plate rack, on top. Then it was bath night and what a performance that was. Two galvanised buckets full of water on the gas cooker, each with a handful of soda crystals added and brought to the boil. This was then transferred to an oblong shaped galvanised receptacle called a hip bath, planted in front of the open fire and a measure of my growing manhood was the increasing ability to carry the buckets of hot water from cooker top to the bath – well, I was quite a big lad, really. Usually, just less than a bucket and a half of cold water added, was enough for a decent depth of nice alluring water. At this stage, with only two of us kids to bath, I was reasonably happy taking the second bath in the same water – perhaps just topped up with a kettle of boiling water for my turn. It was a year or so later, after Ruth had arrived and grown old enough to bathe, when I had to bathe after two girls had done so, leaving a floating scum of soap and talcum powder to penetrate before the water was reached, that really got my back up, as they say but all to no avail, I still had to bathe!

Saturday morning was grocery shopping and bag wash day. Of course, shopping was still something of a nightmare for any mother, because we were still rationed and balancing the money supply, wasn't the only worry as you had to work within the constraints of coupons and rations, as well as the shortage of money. Our nominated grocer was Hetty's, a little Jewish shop quite near to my school and that is where I would go, sometimes all three of us and sometimes just Lillian and me. It was all personal service in this shop and no self-service, but I seem to remember that a lot of things were pre-packaged, with not very many things loose and needing weighing.

Hetty was a wily old shopkeeper, though, as were many of her ilk in those difficult days, with an uncanny ability to advance items against next week's ration, for example and there was always a bit of leeway, you might call it, for a few extra coins and it was called the 'black market' or 'under the counter trading'. This is where my mother's hard-earned money went and why she always worked so hard, mostly with two or more jobs, if one did not pay enough. She spent the money on her kids and her family's needs, rarely on herself and never with an ounce of begrudging. She could never save, only spend, my poor mother and many is the row that my parents had over this issue. Mind you, many were the family altercations over money, that were all the fault of my father, too, when he came home from the Army and more of that later. Suffice to say for now that I can remember my mother commenting to me that had my father been better able to hold his tongue against Army authority, during the whole of his service, he would have held his promotions in rank and correspondingly, his better pay would have reflected in his marriage allowance to my mother back home, with the obvious benefit to her and us.

Continuing with Saturday shopping, no more than a few doors away from Hetty's was the local Sussex Laundry shop and the weekly rendezvous for me and the family washing, taken in a big hessian sack, bleached a creamy white, full of dirty stuff going in and an equally big sack full of clean washed and bleached stuff brought out, to carry back home. It was called the 'bagwash'. Much heavier going home, too, because it was still damp and by the time I reached home, whatever I was wearing was well dampened around the neck and shoulders. Well, I was the growing lad in the family and, therefore, the one to do it but later, I was to make my life much easier and even pleasurable with chores of this nature and errands in general. The proximity of the two shops, the grocers and the laundry, often called for a double trip, a real grind you might say, until my solution to such problems solved such issues.

There was usually one other main errand, which took in two calls each Saturday. The first was to 'Dewhursts', the butcher and the purchase, according to the constraints of the Ration Book, of a rather paltry joint of meat, possibly some scrag-end of lamb and or belly of pork, which Mum would do wonders with. The second call was to 'Funnells', the baker and both places were in the opposite direction to the first two destinations, the grocer and the laundry, but never mind, as I say it would be no problem later. I can't resist owning up to a typical boyish weakness, at this point and that will lead me into digressing slightly, too, but what of it, I'm writing this thing, aren't I? My confession is to digging into the end of the often still warm loaf of bread bought at Funnell's until, by the time one reached home, there was a rather deep and cavernous hole in the once whole loaf – does anyone admit to the same weakness?

The digression is prompted by this naughtiness, highlighting the fact as I recorded in my wartime experience, of my abiding memory of always being hungry, so the same was true of the present times of my narrative, probably because we were still labouring under rationing? Although, I tend to suppose, too, that the reason was a natural characteristic of an active, healthy lad unlikely to be fully fed sometimes and especially with the frugal supplies of the times, despite my mother's extra purchasing efforts. The rest of most Saturdays was playtime and further on you will read more about the things that I got up to which, of course much involved Lillian, my buddy. After my father came home from his war, things would be quite different, not so much during the week as far as my activities were concerned, because he would be off to work from early in the morning, until about 6.30 pm in the evening and that's when he did come home anyway, instead of going on to his two or three nights a week extracurricular activity – dog racing and more of that later. Things changed on Saturdays for me especially because avid following of the Arsenal took over on Saturday afternoons, you see but inevitably things changed in many other ways, too. This was more to do with a stricter regime in the home, basics like less room for us all and especially play room for us kids with Mum and Dad needing privacy, as private as you could get in just three rooms!

The left-hand picture shows the flats, not dissimilar to the ones in which we lived and stretching into the distance, in the right-hand picture. In this picture, just as the pavement ends and the road widens, on the left side of the view, is where Hetty's shop was. A few yards further on, probably about where the walker is in the mid distance, was the Sussex laundry shop.

DAD'S HOMECOMING – FAMILY AGAIN

That was the next big event then, really, my father's homecoming, although as events go, I suppose there had been the street parties after Victory in Europe (VE) day, which I wasn't back home for and then Victory in Japan (VJ) day that did happen after I was back home and I don't remember as being particularly over memorable, not to me, at any rate except for, perhaps, the food and the fun of the day itself. In the street just opposite to our flat, both ends were cordoned off against traffic use. The whole street was adorned with flags, bunting, balloons and red, white and blue streamers. Down the middle of the road an endlessly long trestle table was laid out, with long benches and chairs either side. Side tables were loaded with tea urns, bottles of drink, lemonade, cream soda and such and probably something a bit stronger for the adults. The sitting tables were loaded with, sandwiches, crisps, cakes, pastries, fruit, jellies, blancmange and whatever. Where it all came from, I do not know and didn't really care because it was just great to see it and the accompanying music, fun and games was so therapeutic, after so long being restricted and deprived. I remember the dancing in the streets going on very late in the evening and all our Mums and the locals must have worked so hard, with limited resources and money to organise it all.

Now, getting ready for Dad coming home was something else or was it the imminent return of my sheath knife that created my excitement? Most of the preparation was down to my mother, really and I can only scratch the surface of imagining what it must have been like for her. For over 4 long years she had worked and survived alone, with my sister from a 1 year old upwards, in a constantly dangerous area of London throughout the war, very narrowly escaping death or injury on two occasions by V2 rockets and now, just maybe, she was beginning to relax from the fear and tension of danger albeit still with the heavy responsibility of feeding and providing for a young family. Add to all this the apprehension of her husband soon coming home again and she had only seen him once or twice in over 4½ years. What was life going to be like with her partner that she had learned to manage without, when he finally returned home and took over and would he or how would he even, do that? How different a person would he be after the many dangers and experiences that he had endured and been through himself. Would he be a different man to get to know and live with? So, her preparations were not restricted to just making room for another person and his gear, not just the practical day to day things around the home of an extra person to share with but there were the emotions, the feelings and the prospect of living with him, maybe rediscovering the marriage itself? All of this would have been part and parcel of her preparations, her getting ready. Of course, I would not have had thought of these things at that time – these are the musings of my adult mind many years later.

So, let me digress, to try and describe what Mum's last significant emotional memory about Dad probably was and one most certainly not to be erased by a couple of short exciting leave reunions, in that 4½ year stretch of his absence. I remember her telling me that soon after my father was called up into the Army, after some training postings he was posted to a big camp at Blandford, in Dorset. In distance terms these days, not a problem but then it was like being half a world away. Anyway, Mum was not to be kept away from her man, though and on most weekends, she was off down to Dorset to stay in digs near the camp, often taking Lillian with her, too.(This was before we all ended up in Swindon) My father had been promoted and was an Instructor at the Royal Artillery Gunnery School, so despite not being able to get a pass every time, he still managed to wrangle nipping out of camp unofficially but he was never one to be restricted by rules and regulations, anyway! So, he used to bunk out, stay with Mum in her digs or where she and Lillian were billeted and slip back into camp early next morning. Until, that is, that desperate weekend when Mum waited for him to arrive on the Saturday and he never turned up, nor the next day, Sunday, either. Now Mum could be obstinate, too, so off to the camp she went on the Monday morning, up to the Guard Room at the gate and requested to see her husband. "That was not possible" was the response, but they would gladly relay him a message, so what was his name, number and unit? After a short wait, an Orderly Sergeant came out to see her, confirming that she could not see Dad and to give her his best advice. That was to go home and wait to hear from her husband by letter, because he and his whole regiment had moved out to an embarkation port, somewhere in England, prior to shipping overseas and, no, she could not be told any more than that. What her thoughts and feelings must have been on that dismal journey back to her rented digs can only be imagined but she was, of course, just one of many, many wives who could relate to such a scenario. For instance, in wartime soldiers, sailors and airmen were posted too far and distant places, mostly without warning and all too many did not return, so could that have figured in her thoughts about Dad? I guess you could count on it. Now, over 4½ years later he was coming back and to stay. Does this all sound over the top to some readers and, of course, I did not indulge in such a thought process as a 12-year-old – I'm painting now what I feel must have been the picture then? Well, even if it does sound dramatic in some cases, I am convinced that the majority of families thrown together again after such long periods of separation, struggled immensely!

My personal and urgent preparations were much less deep or complicated for Dad's homecoming! For instance, would Dad finally bring home my sheath knife, what else would he bring, as well, what would happen and how was I to get that "Welcome Home, Dad" sign ready and hung up? To deal with the sign first. It was a sheet of tin, because I reasoned that outside our window on the top floor, if it rained, anything put on paper or cardboard would not survive. Was that an early indication of a later adult, practical, DIY orientated mind, maybe? Similarly, the lettering would have to be done in an oil-based paint or else the colours would run when wet. Where the materials came from or how we afforded them, if they were bought, I'll never know. The sheet of tin was first painted all over in white and then the lettering done in a mid-brown colour – well, Dad was in the Army, wasn't he? The wording you can easily guess but youthful impatience got the better of me and I did not let the whole thing dry, before I lifted it up from lying flat – the result was several 'runs' from several letters! Anyway, with 2 holes punched in each top corner, it was safely and securely tied and suspended just below the windowsill of our top front room window, for all to see? Well, the whole street of residents or passers-by, provided they craned their necks upwards, as they walked along shopping or otherwise, would know that my Dad was coming home from the war, or so I wanted them to know!

Yes, I remember the day when it all happened. I remember us all watching, seemingly endlessly up the street, from our high vantage point and that first sighting of this soldier, kit bag slung across his back, rifle slung on one shoulder and more bags in each hand, clicking his way in studded boots along the street towards us. I seem to remember the excitement of the first moments as we met him at the bottom of our block and later at the surrender of the sheath knife. I remember my Aunt and Uncle coming over from their flat opposite and the neighbours shouting up to us, but I cannot remember great celebrations, though. I wonder why? Was it all an anti-climax or was it just that life at that age is a constant adventure, pressure free and with lots of new and changing things to do, each day?

I seem to remember, too, that this homecoming was my father's final and demobilisation leave before his leaving the Army for good. He would have gone away again, briefly, to surrender his Army gear and be kitted out for Civvy Street, 'demob suit' and all. He soon returned to work, as I seem to remember, and he left home quite early in the morning and then returned home long after us kids and Mum got home in the evening and most times, his dinner was saved on a covered plate and reheated on a saucepan of water on the cooker. His returning home time was going to get later and less predictable, into the evening, as I have already hinted and shall explain later. The dinner was often dried out!

Now, don't get me wrong about the effect that having a father back on the scene had, on me and family life in general. In no way do I want to appear to reduce its' importance or impact. You may well recall that I recorded thinking that my father coming home and all of us being back together, was going to make things 'all right', again. I believe that this became true, especially from the point of view of being a complete family unit and the security aspect of being Mum, Dad and us kids together plus, normal proceedings were soon to be resumed, weren't they and that new sister duly arrived, didn't she? It was my father's returning home present to my mother, my sister Ruth, after his going away gift of 6 years earlier, my sister, Lillian! What I am really getting around to putting on record is the fact that, my father and I never became what you might term great 'buddies'. I respected him then and always did because my upbringing, inbuilt in me would not have allowed otherwise. However, we would never become what you might call, 'feely, touchy or huggy' and that is not meant to be a criticism, just a statement of how it was between us. As a result, all that said, as the years progressed and as my father's outlooks and attitudes to and in life, began to make and leave an impression upon me, I was very hard pressed sometimes to accept or approve of his actions and behaviour.

If that sounds somewhat judgemental or bombastic, I can only put it down to an attempt to explain, in adult terms, what my feelings and thoughts were, as a boy, then a youth and then a man, regarding my father and his status and value in my life. For the present, at 11 years of age, the outline of what I have just tried to expand upon was just that, an outline and very early beginnings and my simplest feelings were to the fore then, such as, I had my sheath knife back as he had promised. As I go on recording my memories, I think the reader will pick up upon some of the happenings that will exemplify the evolving shape of this outline of my meaning and my feelings on this subject.

GRAMMAR SCHOOL AND A NEW SISTER

The major change for me, after Dad returned home from the war, as the family began to settle as a unit etc, was that I changed school and to a grammar school, at that. You will remember that I waltzed through my eleven plus (again, I wonder what happened to Miss Kendrick and if she ever did really get over losing me?) went for my interviews and qualified for the 'A' stream, which I stayed in all through my career at Raine's Foundation Grammar School for Boys, given the full title, founded by Sir Henry Raine in 1719, no less and a fine and long established school tradition that I was to become part of. Not bad, either, for an East End kid from a poor background, wealth wise, that is.

I don't really know how but my forbears, never either financially or materially over-endowed, nevertheless managed to acquire good educational status and were always well presented and groomed. I have no problem either, in declaring or justifying that statement or claim of myself, being entitled to a humble but valid opinion. Of course, I immediately added an extra burden upon my parents stretched income because I needed a uniform, the separate requirements of kit for sports activities and fares for going to and from school plus dinner money. This was a constant nightmare for my father, whose attitude to my new schooling at grammar school and the costs involved, were to be a perpetual gripe for him. As for how I managed it myself, this launch into the grammar school business, well, in my first full term end examinations, I came fourth in form overall, out of 36 pupils and topped the class in French and German so, again, not bad, eh?

For various reasons that may come out in my ramblings, my school record became a little inconsistent, shall we say. I maintained my 'A' stream place and stayed in the top half of the form placings each year, with my worst being twelfth but really, I could have done better, and I know that. One reason for the up and down performance was my growing love of and success in sporting activities. My top preference was for football and every free moment, lunchtimes, mid-morning and afternoon breaks were all devoted to football, usually played with a tennis ball in the school playground. After school we went around to a nearby bombed out school grounds that we had cleared, and we played 'matches' before going home. The school games, however, as with most grammar schools were Rugger and cricket and, although I never went for the latter, I excelled in the former. As a big built lad of almost six feet and around thirteen stone, I was an ideal front row forward and I soon reached the 'house' team level, the school seconds and then the first fifteen quickly followed. The 'house' and school handball team and the athletics field were soon part of my proud achievements, as well, mostly specialising in the shot put, discus and javelin throwing.

In my final two years at school, I won the East London Schools Finals at the shot put and went on to finish fourth, in the All England Schools Finals one year and did the same, throwing the javelin, winning in the East London Finals and then coming sixth in the All England Finals the next year. For the All England Finals, I competed at the White City Stadium, in west London where all the big athletics meetings were held, and I was very proud about that. Especially so because, I was unfortunate enough by about one month, to fall into the senior category each year, so that I was always up against boys up to two years older than myself. With some stronger handling from my father, I believe, the imbalance in my zeal for sporting activity as opposed to academic matters could have been better controlled. His influence amounted to nothing more than to almost ban me from doing homework, claiming that what I did not learn in school, I was not going to learn out of it. I never could fathom that philosophy out and you can imagine the scrapes that it got me into, in respect of poorly or non-completed homework assignments, including the frequent suffering of what is known today as 'corporal punishment' or 4 whacks with the slipper - absolute poppycock, to call it so as I have well commented upon elsewhere!

First founded in 1719, in Shadwell, this is the Raine's Foundation Grammar School building that I went to; for Boys, on the right of centre and Girls, on the left and ne'er the twain shall meet or mix – not in school time, anyway! The immaculate Arbour Square lays in the front. The building is now the home of Tower Hamlets College, the school having transferred to another location.

Things were to change in the home, too, for within 10 months of my fathers' first home leave for demobilisation my sister, Ruth, arrived on the scene. For the reader to have an inkling of what this new arrival meant and increasingly so, as she and Lillian and I grew older, I think that I had better describe in a little detail, something of the size and interior of our flat. From the outside stairs you entered the flat, through the front door, straight into our kitchen, a room about 7 to 8 feet wide by about 9 feet long. At the opposite end of the kitchen to the front door, a glass partition and door led out onto a cast-iron railed balcony and on which was a waist level coal cupboard on one side and a door into a toilet, on the other. From the door out from the kitchen to the railings was about 4 feet. This combined area was adjoined by another room, the size of the kitchen and balcony together in length and about the same in width ie 7 to 8 feet by 13 feet, which was a back bedroom and these two areas were the back of the flat. Right across the total width of these two rooms, in the front of the flat and overlooking the street, was what we called the front room and was probably some 15 feet by 10 feet and with the doors that led into the back bedroom and opened into the kitchen. For a visual idea of all of this, a reference back to Page 90 and the twin external pictures of our flat, viewed from the front and from the rear will help. With 2 adults, my parents, a growing lad and 2 children in residence, you will appreciate that we were not over blessed with space. So, as the birth of my sister became imminent, my parents had vacated what was their bedroom, the back one and us kids, Lillian and I, with our 2 single beds, normally in the front room, were moved into the back for the confinement – whatever that was or meant, to me, in those innocent days?

So now, on the 'fateful' night, I remember waking up at what time I have no idea, after being packed off to bed early and hearing all this commotion going on in the front room and it sounded quite frightening! My sister woke up, too and asked me what was happening and why all the hubbub and noise in the other room? Now how in heavens name did I know what was happening? We kept hearing my mother talking quite loudly and she sounded, at times, as though she was moaning. Was she in pain, ill or something and where was Dad, couldn't he see to her? Maybe he had gone for the doctor? Should I go and see what was wrong? Then I heard my grandmother's voice, too, so what was she doing here? Maybe I'll stay put, I thought, if Gran was there, she would sort it as she was a nurse (a midwife, but I wouldn't have known the difference then or its' appropriateness to the situation) Then another woman's voice, in a very strong tone saying, "Bear down, Mrs. Chambers, bear down!" I suppose that that must have been the District Nurse, because we had lots of visits from her in the following weeks. Well, how long this all went on for I cannot remember but Lillian and I were pretty shook up by all this, because whatever was happening was pretty serious, by the sound of it.

Finally, after another bout of moans and groans and commands of "Bear down" there was another cry – a baby cry! So that was it, our little brother or sister that we had been told was coming any day had arrived. Where from we had no idea and why in the middle of the night and why make such a noise and fuss about it? We both really did not have a clue about all the intricacies of childbirth. Can you imagine trying to convince anybody of such a scenario these days? Why, a child barely able to talk would be able to give chapter and verse nowadays on what was proceeding. I was only almost

12 years old, after all, so what would I know about such things in that day and age? Anyway, Ruth was now with us and my chores were soon going to extend to nursery activities, as well, including lots of different things on the shopping lists. In latter days, I mischievously remind my 'baby' sister from time to time that her nappy changing was soon to be listed among my household and family attributes, as well!

Mum and Dad went back into the rear bedroom, with Ruth's cot added and Lillian and I returned to our makeshift beds in the front room. Later, as Ruth got older and bigger, we had a settee that we folded down each night into a double bed and the girls slept on there. As for me, I just slept each night on what was known as a Zed Bed, a fold-down bed, in the kitchen. As we all washed at the sink each morning, in a corner of the kitchen, this meant that I was always the first up and as the kitchen was always in use, also the last to go to bed at night. Amusingly, as an aside to my sleeping on this bed, I can recall that from time to time we were plagued with mice. I used to put any loose coins from my trouser pocket and my handkerchief on the floor under the bed, when I laid down to sleep. One night I awoke to the chinking of coins – it was a mouse playing in my handkerchief and running back and forth over the coins on the floor!

INNOVATION AND D.I.Y. INSTINCTS BLOSSOM

I think that it would be opportune now to expand on some of the things that I have hinted of, in my narrative and which were very much part of my everyday life. For instance, the early signs of practical abilities that would blossom in later years into very competent DIY skills. A prime example of this was my home made, wooden scooter. The reader should not be at all disillusioned by this basic description because this scooter or my version, was the best example of this form of transport in the East End and was no 'Heath Robinson' contraption. Conversely, it was a soundly constructed, highly versatile and technically advanced piece of mobility kit and it featured dual handlebars for cruising and speed racing; an anti-slip foot board, a rear wheel braking system, a front headlamp (from a bicycle) and a detachable side-car, no less! The last mentioned I could have patented, I believe, because I never came across another example of a scooter with a side-car, anywhere. Lots of kids had these self-made scooters because we certainly could not have afforded to buy things like this, even if available but I perfected the art, you might say. As you can guess, we also painted them various colours and otherwise decorated and embellished them – I nailed coloured bottle tops to the front of mine in a fancy pattern, for instance. Before I tell of what practical uses besides the recreational purpose that this machine was put to, I have attempted to sketch an impression of what it looked like but whether my feeble effort will achieve that aim, remains to be seen.

Sketch of home made scooter

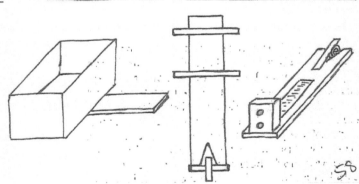

Hopefully, at least, you should be able to recognise the component parts and then visualise what the assembled whole looked like. The riding board, on the right shows the rear brake, which was pressed down on to the rear wheel by the foot. The block at the front had two large screw eyes, which then located with two similar ones on the back of the upright, front or steering board (centre sketch) and through all four screw eyes was passed a long, sturdy bolt with a retaining nut on the end. Thus, the two boards were firmly connected and swivelled to enable the front to steer and note the two positioned handlebars, the upper one for cruising and the lower for racing, ensuring that you crouched lower, as you propelled yourself along with your free leg – aerodynamics you understand, less wind resistance! An ex bicycle lamp was fixed near the top between the two handlebars. The two wheels were a large (approx. 4 inch) wheel-bearing race for the front and a smaller sized one for the rear. The purchase of such bearings brought a sales upsurge to the ironmongery stores of my day, called Robert Dyas's, as did the need for large strong bolts and screw eyes.

The box contraption (left-hand sketch) was none other than my side-car on one end and the other end of the protruding plank was located on the foot- board, of the scooter and bolted through with removable bolts. At the box end of the plank, under the box itself was another wheel-bearing to take the weight of the side-car and contents, which could be the shopping or my sister as a passenger. So, you see, today's aluminium examples of recent years, were not a new concept and nowhere near as versatile or useful – they should have asked me! You might wonder, at this point, about my bicycle, the purchase of which I told you all about earlier? Well, I still had it and used it a lot around the streets of London but, unfortunately, I had a rival for its' usage – my father! The reasons for this I shall explain as we progress.

Now I have revealed how, many of the chores and errands that I was responsible for, became so much easier and enjoyable. That scooter, like my bicycle of some years previous, became part of me and I went everywhere on it and so did my shadow, my sister, Lillian – the prime reason why I needed the side-car? I can also now link the reader with the reference, some pages back, to Aldgate Pump as being the place where the 'asphalt pavements began' and here's the explanation and reason why! These pavements were heavenly for ball-bearing wheels to run over, so much smoother and quieter to ride on and better grip than over the stone paving slabs and the judder, judder of the joins between the slabs. For some unknown reason, all of the pavements in the City area of London were of this smooth asphalt and with the exodus of almost all pedestrians (office workers) at the end of each day, these pavements became our thoroughfares and race tracks for the scooters each evening and all over the weekend. A goodly number of those bombsite paradises (to us they were, anyway) were in the city, especially around the Moorgate, St. Paul's and Lower Thames Street areas and the scooter was our transport to and from. Incidentally, I will record here, as an adjunct to the absence of pedestrian's phenomena in the City, the fact that it really is a lovely and fascinating place for just walking and exploring, on a summer evening or at the quiet weekend. All the streets, alleys and byways of the greatest and most wonderful City on this planet, London. I am biased, of course, but right nevertheless and you can take my word for it – the walking if not the bias!

From the crossroads with Wentworth Street, our street named Goulston Street, went up a slight incline for a little over 100 yards or so before levelling off, on its' way to Aldgate High Street, at the top. The reverse direction, therefore, made it an ideal short racetrack for running races but mostly bikes or scooters and, would you believe it, the surface was that wonderful smooth asphalt. This reminds me, too, of one of those 'old wives tales' perpetuated by my mother and grandmother. They both maintained that should we ever see the council workmen repairing or patching the roads or pavements, laid with the smooth asphalt of which I write, then we were to stand and inhale the fumes from the hot buckets of tar and asphalt, boiling over hot coal fires, before being spread and levelled by hand, by the workmen on their knees. It was good for the lungs and, especially if you had a cold, they always said. I have spent many a long wait doing this and know the whole work process from clearing the broken surfacing, then the hole filling, to the final patching and laying plus finishing with fine sand, dusted in to the surface but I watched just to inhale the fumes, you see! Now, you do not have to believe me, but I never remember losing a race whether it was running, cycling or scootering that was involved – you just did not outdo Eddie Chambers in these pursuits! So much, then, for my methods of transport and the movement from place to place going for errands and in play and fun.

Just to prove my point, this is an East End street scene of a scooter race, showing two boys on homemade wooden scooters. Much inferior to mine, of course but the one mid picture (not the leader) is similar and you can make out the ballbearing wheels on both.

THE NEIGHBOURHOOD: MY STREET AND ITS' VARIOUS ACTIVITIES

The location and environment of these times of my childhood were, of course, what we term nowadays as 'inner city' and slums at that. I never saw it that way, by any measure. This was my world, just as much as the more country-like life of Upminster had become but I doubt very much if it could have been or I could have done the same in reverse, if I had come from the country. Now my street was a market for 6 days of the week. A local, busy one from Monday to Friday and a packed seething mass of humanity, that extended over several streets on each Sunday – the world-famous Petticoat Lane!

Saturday was in between, and it was dead and not the least of reasons being that Saturday was the Jewish Sabbath or 'Shabbos'. On each of the market days, there were also a variety of shops open, being all the street level premises topped by the occupied flats above them, including ours.

In my street there was a café, two grocers, a butcher, a couple of dress shops, several wholesalers of rolls of tailors and dressmakers' materials and a milliner. Additionally, on each of the weekdays, there were a dozen or so stalls whose sole trading was chickens, well, hens mostly. Just two streets away were the official 'Beth Din' controlled, slaughterhouses for the poultry trade, so much part of the Jewish business life in the area. The poultry came in from farms, their commercial egg laying days over, in crates and then slaughtered in their many thousands. Many went to food processors to be used in the manufacture of chicken paste, chicken soup etc but many found their way to the retail poultry sellers. At each of the stalls in our street men and women sat, plucking hens, cleaning and gutting them and selling them to shoppers. The upper frames of the stalls hung heavy with un-eviscerated carcases and wooden tea chests were used, to store the entrails in during the day and a constant pungent smell filled the air. At the end of each day the refuse lorry and a team of street cleaners would be followed by the "water cart" which high pressure sprayed and disinfected the whole street. The following picture, illustrates exactly what I have just described about the stalls and you can only imagine what it was like to work on them, freezing in the winter and stinking, as well as stifling hot, in summer and even more smelly! This is what my street was like during every weekday, then quite clear on Saturdays, followed by the huge market on Sundays.

This picture was taken before the war in 1937, so nothing changed to when I remember it in the mid 1940's. The man standing, and plucking is, apparently, a Phil Solomon the stall owner and the woman sitting, I recognise as one who was doing the same job when I lived there. She was known as 'Lily Chickens' so her life had changed little in those 10 years. It appears that the lady whose head is immediately above Lily's, is that of my Uncle Leslie's mother-in-law to be, some 5 years or so after this picture was taken. Notice the scales for weighing the fowls and those hanging up, plus the empty tea chest for the feathers and entrails etc!

On a Sunday, things were different, and I described the streets a few sentences back as a seething mass of humanity, as the pictures of it confirm and Petticoat Lane market spread through Wentworth Street, Goulston Street (my street) New Goulston Street, Middlesex Street and parts of Gravel Lane and Harrow Place. From around late morning on Saturday, teams of workers would bring out, from store sheds, barrow loads of trestles, planks, steel stanchions, heavy stall tables and rolled up canvas sheet covers. From all this material, rows of stalls would be erected on either side of the streets, each with a 'pitch number' and on which the stallholder would hang his 'Licence to Trade'. By the evening all the empty stalls would be in place, ready for early occupation by traders on Sunday morning and the previous picture clearly illustrates the finished erected stall. As you will read later, I speak with first-hand experience of the, what was known as, 'stalling out' process and the packing up as 'stalling in'. The following picture also illustrates my point about the stall's layout and the seething mass of humanity.

This is looking east, from Middlesex Street, along the length of Wentworth Street. Along the right-hand side of the street, in the distance, can be made out a clock high on the wall, which was above Paul's dress shop. A few yards past that, going off to the right is my street, Goulston Street and this junction is the bottom of the incline, which was our bike and scooter 'racetrack'.

CHARACTERS OF 'THE LANE'

When I first returned to London, my father came back from the war and we began to settle in as a family, Lilian and I were often roaming spectators of and in the Sunday morning Petticoat Lane market. We would wander around in between the stalls, watch the demonstrators promoting their wares: the special 'stay sharp' kitchen knives, the magic window cleaners, wonder non-stick pans, amazing stain removers, paint-brush cleaners etc, etc. The stall that I used to spend hours watching at, was the one that demonstrated the toy 'gyroscope', like a spinning top that travelled along wires, round the rims of glasses, stood on the end of a pencil and so on and never fell off or over, spinning for minutes on end. Then there was that amazing bloke who sold china and crockery off about three stalls joined together and had a team of assistants, milling around in front of him, to serve and take money and some others stationed in the crowd, as 'dummy' buyers to get things moving when the offers or deals were shouted out. He was a born juggler with plates, cups, saucers, tureens and all sorts flashing from one hand to another and often ending up piled up and balancing on one hand and ne'er a sign of a broken piece. The incredible quickfire, colourful sales patter was something that had to be heard to be believed and this was before the 'spivs' and 'wide-boys' of the 1950's and 60's. I can still hear it all now and I spell it as it sounded! "'Ere you are, lady. I tell ya wot I'll do. Dere's a set o' dinner crocs (holding a stack of plates and tureens in one hand) Wot did I say, free quid a set? Right, 'Ere's wot I'll do. Dere's anuver set. Not six quid, not five an'arf quid, not even five – dere you are two sets, four an' arf quid! Nar, 'oo wants 'em? Dere's one over dere, nuver one down 'ere. Ain't it good, eh? 'Old on there guv'ner, my mates coming, just stay dere!" The patter would carry on, "Don't go away, lady, it's ya birfday, look wot I got 'ere, your 'ole man'll bless you when you git 'ome!" The crowds laughed and enjoyed the entertainment, even if they bought nothing and especially when they heard the words, "*'Ere, did ya 'ear the one about the bloke on the No. 8 bus?*" A smutty joke was then on its way and they all loved it!

Another incredible showman was the bloke who sold bedding; pillows, sheets, blankets, curtains, towels, tea towels and so on. He would grab individual sheets or towels etc and toss them way out into the crowd for them to 'feel the quality', to be caught by a planted stooge who would do his bit and then "buy" 2 or 3. When he put together his 'multiple buy deals' he often disappeared behind this mound of bedding and whatever that he was holding but you could still hear his voice. A favourite spiel was always that there was only a limited supply that this was the last of the stock and these were never to be repeated offers, except if you came back next week, hey presto, there they all were again!

Then there were the street photographers with their tripod cameras, with the developing and fixing fluids in containers attached to the legs of the tripod – the forerunners of the Polaroid cameras, I suppose. They would stop you in your tracks whilst taking your picture, tell you how wonderful you looked, talking all the time whilst dipping the film in the pots to develop and print and finally waving this brown or sepia coloured picture in front of you for you to purchase. It was all too easy to be conned or talked into letting go of your money for something that you did not want, and you don't know how you fell for it, but you did! To roam the market, you needed to be on your guard constantly and guard your belongings, even those fastened to you. The tale is often told, with little exaggeration, of how you could have your watch, or some jewellery 'lifted' from you at one end of the market and offered to you for sale at the other end! But that's like all markets, I suppose and, like all markets it was colourful, entertaining, absorbing and a real education about life, for those living and growing up in such a diverse environment.

Back now to those characters of 'The Lane' and a little about those special individual characters that frequented most markets and were there to dazzle, entertain, exploit and swindle you but in a way that left you either outraged,

178

fuming, amused, flabbergasted and sometimes even quietly admiring, for their cheek, audacity and sheer personality. I have already mentioned a couple of the 'traders' or stall characters juggling and bandying merchandise, but these were different, the celebrities you might say or the star attractions – the ones that you went to see just for themselves, as well as spending your money on bargains. I'll just pick on three to elaborate upon my point.

The first were the beigel sellers, Esther (I never knew her second name!) and Annie Allwinkle. My mother went to school with Annie and often used to say 'hello' when she saw her in the streets. You'll notice the way that I have spelt 'beigel?' I know not which the grammatically correct way is but I know how we all spelt it in my day and I do know that today's modern 'bagel', is not the beigel that I knew and that Esther and Annie sold. We loved their variety, especially filled with slices of smoked salmon and cream cheese. Both ladies carried huge wicker baskets full of beigels, a supply of brown paper bags to put them in, with their money pouch under a flowing coat and often just squatting on a small stool on the street corner. Otherwise they somehow had these big baskets slung across their shoulders and hanging in front of them, just trawling their way along until all the beigels were sold. I think it was Esther who provided the entertaining part to her character by quoting her own made up poetry, as she called out her sales pitch and I clearly can remember that two of her 'offerings' went like this...

"Beigels for the rich, beigels for the poor. When I've sold out you can't 'ave no more!", *"Beigels for the Navy, beigels for the Army, beigels for the clever and beigels for the balmy!"*

The following picture shows both in situ, although not in the 'Lane'. It might have been in Brick Lane and it's ironic that a 24-hour Bagel shop thrives in the same street today, although the rest of the businesses and residents are Bangledeshi, both original emigrants and those since born here. Esther is in the foreground and Annie on the other corner, whom my mother went to school with. Notice the wicker basket and the small round 'beigels' – not the so-called 'bagels' of today!

Then there was this 'Houdini' type character, an escapologist whose name I never knew, and his speciality was escaping from all sorts of bound and tied up situations. I often used to walk to the top of Tower Hill, by the Tower of London itself, to see this chap perform but the Sunday Petticoat Lane market was another favourite venue. No doubt there were many little tricks to his act, but he would be handcuffed; bound hand and foot with rope, sometimes his whole body bound, then blindfolded, wrapped in sacking, shackled with chains or tied to a chair, lashed to planks of wood – the task of freeing himself, seemingly out of the question! Wrong! Our man always made it!

To aid authenticity, people from the watching crowd were invited to help with the binding process, lock the padlocks on the chains or inspect knots etc but whether they were 'planted' or not, I can only guess. There was always a good rain of coins to fill the flat cloth cap on the ground after the performance. I can remember often feeling sorry for this poor chap, who was always poorly dressed, nearly always in shabby trousers and sleeveless singlet vest, no socks or shoes, he never spoke and always looked utterly miserable and despairing. All the commentary and binding up was done and supervised by his sidekick, who spun it out, for a good five or ten minutes, before the actual 'escaping' act began. I'll bet they both went home in a Rolls Royce hidden away somewhere.

A piece of waste ground for a stage and a passing audience this time, as opposed to a watching crowd in the markets, or on Tower Hill.

Before I go on to my last favourite character, I can't quite remember if another 'Houdini' chap was one and the same person or not, but I favour it being another but very similar showman type act. This time it was strength, sheer superhuman strength, that was on show. He would take thick London telephone books and agonise over gradually ripping them in half – as a complete book with his bare hands. There was undoubtedly a knack to it and some said that the books were doctored beforehand, by being baked in an oven to make the paper brittle. Whatever, it was certainly entertaining but did not end there, because this chap would go on to bend iron bars across his forehead, the back of his neck and over his knee. This was usually followed by fire breathing, some acrobatics, rope walking and weight lifting feats, like lifting chairs with stooges from the watching crowd sitting on them, by a rope clenched in his teeth, pulling through a pulley. If it was entertainment that you came for, then 'The Lane' provided it in good measure, on a Sunday morning!

Thirdly, the most colourful of the lot, and he was grandly called Prince Monolulu. Now there was a character to behold, very tall, African I believe, resplendent in colourful, flowing robes, long bright boa round his neck, feathers sticking out of a headdress and a fistful of racing cards and printed tips for all the horse race meetings – he was a famous tipster. He attended many of the race courses all over but on non-racing days, he could be found at venues like Petticoat Lane and always had a good following as he swept almost regally along the street - after all, was he not a Prince? He often carried a huge coloured umbrella and his famous cry was, again I spell it as it sounded! *"Arr gotta harse, arr gotta harse!"* I can't remember how much he charged for his list of tips, most probably because I wasn't into betting myself but was still fascinated by the Prince and his following.

I don't know where the feathers or coloured umbrella (his black one is there) have got to but he seems in full cry: "Arrr..." or perhaps the "harse" bit exiting his mouth.

They are the three characters that I have chosen as my favourites but there were many more. The constant prattle of human conversations and typical, quickfire, cockney chatter, the banter and repartee were a whole captivating entertainment experience, as well. As in the 1950's and moving into the 1960's you can just imagine these places being a working paradise for 'spivs', 'wide boys', petty crooks and small-time gangsters. Come rain or shine, the 'Lane' was the place to be on a Sunday and, later, I will describe what it was like to work, on a stall, in the Sunday Petticoat Lane market frequented by all classes and with an atmosphere and aura all to itself.

ON THE STREET WHERE I LIVED

What you have just read about, is what my street was like on a Sunday until around 2.00pm, when the 'stalling in' period would begin, the street cleaners would descend on the area, the rubbish lorries would be loaded and the 'water cart' would do its' spraying and disinfecting job and all the while the stall clearing team was tearing around to get stalls dismantled and the materials back in storage. Come the late afternoon and Sunday peace descended at last on Petticoat Lane! So, you see, my street was world famous – everyone knew or had heard of 'Petticoat Lane'. It was unique for other reasons, too. It had a large cinder, cycle racing track (car park, really!) it had a Public Baths, an indoor swimming pool, a roadside loading and holding area, for big wheeled carts pulled by pairs of those huge, beautifully groomed animals, Clydesdale horses, for the Brooke Bond Tea Company. Then, two jellied eel stalls at the Aldgate end, none other than Mitchell's and Tubby Isaacs. What a thoroughfare to boast as being, in the words of the song, "*on the street where we lived*".

But I had better provide some descriptive explanation for my readers to appreciate this last paragraph. So first, I'll explain the cycle track. Earlier in this collection of memories, I described the awful events of the Friday afternoon when a V2 rocket fell in my street, opposite the Public Baths, as later told to us by my mother, who was there. The large area of devastation caused by this tragedy had been turned into an extension of Petticoat Lane, for stalls on Sundays and as a car parking area, during the week. The whole area was levelled and compacted by heavy rollers and covered by cinders, also then heavy rolled. In the middle of this area all of us, the kids of the neighbourhood, would lay out a cycle speedway track, using bricks to mark a perimeter, just like the craze sport of that era, motorcycle speedway. We would tear round this track, trying to copy the rear wheel sliding action of the motorbikes at each corner. Yours truly excelled on his solid Hercules roadster bicycle but you had to get a real burst of speed up, on the 'straights', to get enough impetus to be able to stop peddling, lean over, hang out a leg and slide the back-wheel round. The tyres took a hammering, too, but it was all great fun!

Then there were those Clydesdale horses. "What?" you say, "in a London street, surely, they were for pulling ploughs in fields?" Opposite the open space and the cycle track, on the other side of the road and next to the Public Baths, was a large building with a sizeable loading space in front, where the road was also widened. There were several shuttered loading bays at street level, of this very large warehouse, the London Distribution Depot of Brooke Bond, the well-known brand of tea - you know, 'Divi or Dividend' and 'P.G. Tips' etc. Well now, much of the delivery and movement of product, for several years just after WW2, was by horse-drawn carts and this is where those wonderful Clydesdales featured. I have been unable to track down any photos of these animals in action, as Brooke Bond 'employees' but the way that they manoeuvred those big drays, mastered by their drivers was incredible.

The road was typically made of the familiar granite cobblestones and these big heavy creatures often struggled for their footing, especially when reversing. The road surface was well sanded, mind you, for this very reason. The other thing that made the sight so impressive was the immaculate turnout of both drays and animals. The paintwork sparkled on wheels and framework, the harness of which there was plenty, and the long reins were all shiny black, the brass accoutrements just glistened, the coats, manes and tails of each pair of horses were brushed immaculately and their hooves highly polished black and they were a sight to see, that's for sure. I vividly remember passing them all lined up along the road, on my way up to catch the bus for school and often used to fear that one of them would take a nip at me, as I had to walk so close to them – they were like elephants to me and I was more at ease when they had their nose bags on, feeding. By the way, one also had to be quick and nimble when one chose the wrong time to go past the horses, like just as they decided to pass water or something more solid even! I think the words waterfall and avalanche spring to mind and the pavement was not very wide, either, as I have already indicated. However, all of this went the way of progress, the horses solid, built like tanks, went away and Trojan vans took over the delivery duties. I found a picture of real Trojans and one of a Dinky Toy model, in Brooke Bond Tea livery. Then best of all, a picture of Trojan vans all lined up outside the Brooke Bond warehouse, in our street.

A picture of Trojan vans in various liveries – probably a company photo and one of a Dinky model.

THE BROOKE BOND WAREHOUSE IN GOULSTON STREET

To the left of the large lorry starts the building housing the baths and the swimming pool. At the bottom right corner of the picture is a private car, parked in the cinder laid car park now surrounded by the low wall, also visible. This car park was the site of the V2 rocket hit that had wreaked havoc in the market, some 150 yards away to the left of this picture and in the baths and pool opposite. It was also where we had our post war cinder cycle speedway track. By the way, can you imagine those delivery vans being horse-drawn drays, instead of Trojan vans?

So, to the jellied eel stalls. There are several long established hot pie and mash and eels and mash eating houses in the East End, like Cooke's and Manzie's that date back to the 1800's and that served this traditional East Enders' fare. Both Mitchell's and Tubby Isaacs, the two jellied eel stalls at the Aldgate end of our street also had a very long family history. The Mitchell's stall was on one corner, the same corner that was the original site of Aldgate East station, before the new station was opened some 100 yards or so further along. On the other corner, outside what was in my day 'The Fifty Shilling Tailors', later 'John Colliers', was Tubby Isaacs's stall. Their offering was different with the eels cooked and served cold in jelly, in little china dishes, which you ate with a hunk of crusty bread and lashings of pepper and vinegar – to my mother and I quite delicious but I accept that they were and are an acquired taste. I say 'are' because I still indulge even though I live now in Folkestone, Kent. Down at the old harbour there are several fish stalls, one of which is run by an ex East London family, selling all kinds of shellfish etc, including the celebrated Jellied Eels – yes!

I digress – back to Mitchell's and Tubby Isaacs. The stalls were part of the street 'furniture', you might say, and I can never remember them not being there and open for business and well into the early hours of the morning, almost certainly, although I think they were closed when I went past on my way to school each morning! They sold other shell fish, of course, cockles, mussels, winkles and whelks all being favourite EastEnders' fare – most especially on the way home from the pub, the 'pictures' (cinema) or any other evening outing. My mother also often used to send me up to the top of our street for a tub of eels, which had to have the vinegar and pepper added and with the chunk of plain white bread but purchased from Tubby Isaacs only!

A picture of Tubby Isaacs's Jellied Eels stall taken in the 1950's, outside John Collier's (formerly Fifty Shilling Tailors)

Finally, the Public Baths incorporating the indoor swimming pool which was only 25 yards long and the big commercial laundry, behind these afore mentioned buildings. The first point to note is that a laundry had occupied that site for some 200 years, but the other facilities came later. The second newsworthy note is that this is the baths complex, opposite which that V2 rocket fell on other buildings, with such an awful carnage resulting and the consequent cleared area giving way to the cinder car park/cycle speedway track already described. I refer here, of course, to the scene of my mother and sister's experience described in the first part of my writings, when I was prevented from making my usual weekend visit from Upminster to see them.

So, you see, that was the street where and on which I lived. I often think of how many stories and interesting street and road descriptions could and have been be recorded, from individual experiences all over the world and especially childhood ones. So many different towns, cities, villages and communities, in different countries, hot and cold climates etc and most interestingly where significant or dramatic circumstances formed the backdrop to those stories – it just needs to be written down! Just one last note about my street is, that everything described thus far applied to the stretch from our flats, to the Aldgate end of the street. The other end led to another famous market, that would feature greatly in my latter adult life, the largest covered wholesale fruit and vegetable market in the world – Spitalfields Market.

Still under the general heading of the streets and the area in which I lived, it is true to say that because of the proximity to the huge London Docks complex, many cosmopolitan influences made their mark on the area. The Docks themselves with the wharf workers and the 'closed shop' stevedores, the Flemish weavers, the Jewish garment and tailoring trades and many warehousing and storage companies, employing all kinds of migrant workers and labourers etc all contributed to the colour, the class levels, the living standards and the diversity of employment and unemployment, come to that! The narrow streets, the

189

tenement blocks, poor housing, the street 'ladies', petty crime, the 'live by your wits' culture and sheer poverty were all to be found, in the area, coming up to and around the turn of the century.

A lot of it changed as a result of WW2 with whole streets and communities totally disfigured or destroyed but the legacies of the past remained, as did the history and reputation. None more so than the memory of the fact that this was 'Jack the Ripper' country! Incredibly, three of the homes that I lived in, were located within yards and four others very close to, the sites of horrific murders attributed to this elusive character and still they remain unsolved to this day. The closest, in George Yard, Gunthorpe Street, was at the end of the turning where College Buildings was situated – a walk of no more than 50/60 yards from our front gates! However, it had all happened about 50 years before I lived in College but the murders, starting as they did in 1888, were when my grandparents were growing up. They came to live in College Buildings, so close to the scene of that first murder, around 1908, I believe. There is another interesting fact that is worth noting, though, about the diverse standard of dwellings erected in the area around this time and often almost alongside each other.

College Buildings were probably erected around some 10 years or so after the time of Jack the Ripper. The George Yard buildings that were already there then and in which the first horrific murder was committed were slum dwellings, occupied by all and sundry and not supervised in any way, open to all intruders and easily accessed. Whereas, all the tenants of flats in College Buildings were all vetted families or occupants, who had to supply two non-family references and evidence of the ability to pay their rents before tenancy was granted; the building was supervised and secured by a Caretaker, my Grandfather and the sole access was by three iron gated entrances, all locked by Grandad at around 10.00 pm. Late returning residents had to use their key to get back in. What a difference in standards and the class of resident and in almost adjoining premises.

190

This was my London, my East End and apart from the period of the war years, in Upminster, was where I was to live, to be further educated, to grow up, to be married, to have children and expand my life from, for many of the years to follow. I shall digress again, here, to touch upon what I feel were the comparisons between the life experience of my parents and what was to transpire for me. I suppose that the major differences between my parents' generation and mine could be polarised in the areas of travel and lifestyle, much influenced by better education (although this was still somewhat stunted for me) diversity of opportunity and greater job and employment achievements. In addition, the growth, regeneration and new creations plus massive change that were to follow on from a world war, altered the landscape and prospects in life enormously.

On lifestyle, for instance, my parents never owned a house that they lived in and did not own a car until they were almost 60 years old. I don't think that my father ever really grasped the reality gap and difference, either between his own experience, of never rising above basic supervisory level in his building trade career and a top salary of some £3,500 p.a., to that of his son, being a company Managing Director on some £30,000 p.a. (1980) with big company car (plus one of his own) plush office and expenses allowance etc, and that was long before I was in my fifties.

Nor of both his daughters doing so well in business with one also reaching senior management level in the highly competitive retail world. As far as travel was concerned my father had travelled to other parts of the world, courtesy of the Army and in the service of his country. He had never flown in an airplane, always maintaining that if we were meant to fly, God would have given us wings! My parents did get to own a small Ford Popular car in their 60's and managed to travel on camping holidays to Europe. However, after my mother passed away, Dad also did come with us to Australia on holiday and stayed on with my second wife's family for several years, which he loved. The rest of my family had barely travelled beyond the South of England, whereas we now spread our wings to foreign climes on holidays, business trips and flights that my earlier family generations would only have dreamed about. So, just those two topics illustrate very clearly some of the comparisons and differences between us. Certainly, a lifestyle and status level not expected of an East End kid of their era but, as they say, 'the times, they were a-changing!' But I must slow down, we are forging too far ahead. Back we go to my progress into my teenage years, the 'Lane', family things and issues, growing pains and on into the business world, the Royal Air Force and further – well, maybe?

Before I go any further, though, into that range of subjects, let me carry on from my meanderings about Petticoat Lane to relate what it was like to work in the 'Lane', as I said I would, because the experience of 'work' started very early, for me. So how did that come about when I was only 12/13 years old and still a Grammar School boy? I need to digress yet again, just a little, to explain the family view or should I say, my father's view, on matters financial, because that will go a long way to answer the question as to how I became employed at such a tender age. You may remember, too, that I have referred earlier that I would expound on issues that would explain why certain regimes and circumstances became commonplace in my family history. My father, as also explained elsewhere, had been denied further education and any vocational training at 14 years of age, in order to go to work to help support his family, when his father died. At some stage, in the pursuit of more money, he took to gambling and this addiction stayed with him for all his life, with varying degrees of severity and consequence.

The fragile job market of the 1930's, the cruel interruption of WW2 and the difficult post war times that we were now in, made employment progress and the consequent better wage benefits very hard to come by. Consequently, when he was demobbed after the war, although he did go straight into work, in his profession of 'costing' in the building trade, his wages were low and his prospects poor, without the qualifications that were demanded to become, for instance, a Quantity Surveyor. Ironically, as is often the case in the work place, my father's ability (not his qualifications, mind you) and long years of experience in a trade that he never left, equipped and enabled him to do the job, as an example, of a Quantity Surveyor but without the rewards of a qualified operator. For him then, it was all too easy to slip back into the culture of 'chance', by gambling on the dogs, mostly, but also on the horses and an avid football pools fan. As everyone knows and knew, including my Dad if he was honest, there are only winning bookies, not winning punters! My poor old Dad was always convinced that the 'jackpot' would land one day and, I have to say, his declared motivation was always so that he could give his family a better life. That was the background to his insistence on me the eldest child and a son at that, to contributing to family finances, at the earliest possible opportunity. He had been forced to as a child and because of circumstances and present needs, this demanded that history was repeated, in his view. My digression is over, and I hope that you grasp my reasons of repeated digression from the subject in hand?

One day, on my way home from school, a rotund Jewish man stopped me as I was just entering the entrance to my block of flats. His name was Joe Goldberg, whom I knew as did most people in the Lane because he had a flourishing business selling suitcases, attaché cases, cabin trunks, bags, holdalls, briefcases and such like, off a stall at the corner of our street and Wentworth Street – a prime spot in the Lane all week and especially so on a Sunday. He lived in the next block to us and rented the basement flat of the block as storage for all his stock.

These two photos illustrate me at around 10 years old, in the school photo on the left and about 12 to 13 on a day outing, on the right. I cannot remember where to, with Dad on the left and my Uncle Charlie on the right. Note the dress code, for me as mentioned elsewhere in my stories and the formality of the adults, even on an outing to the seaside!

Joe had decided that this biggish strapping lad that he used to see so often, was just what he was looking for, to help him 'stall out' and 'stall in' every day and work the whole of the Sunday Market, too. I will comment here, too, that the following scenario described, also conveniently 'overlooked' my parent's belief and my whole family practice that Sunday was the Lord's Day. So then, here was Joe's proposed deal. I would 'stall out' before going to school in the morning and I had to leave for school by 8.30am. Then straight home from school, at about 4.30pm I would have to get back to 'stall in'. Both exercises, involved carrying all the stock up, or down, the two flights of steps from the basement and along the street, about 50/60 yards to the stall which, during the week, amounted to about 50 pieces, carrying a maximum of 4 at a time, one in each hand and one under each arm. With the cabin trunks, it was only one at a time because they were almost as big as me and for my wages for each day, morning and evening sessions, Monday to Friday, I would be paid 1/- or 5p in today's currency – 5 shillings (25p) per week!

Now Sunday, that was a whole different ball game, and this was how my Sunday went. Joe would expect me down, outside the stockroom at 6.30am to do what I have previously described, only on Sundays I carried anything up to 200 pieces of luggage to the stall. The trade was that much more intense and the volume of sales that much greater and it was hard work, I can tell you. I usually finished stalling out by about 8.30am when I could go for my breakfast. First, though, I went around to the paper shop to get the newspapers for Dad and me, to read all about Arsenal in the football season or Middlesex in the cricket season. Why these two teams? I'll tell you later. Sometimes I had to get bread or milk, too and then chase upstairs to make Mum and Dad tea in bed and cook my breakfast, as we always had an egg and bacon breakfast on Sunday's. Then it was back down to the stall by 9.30 am the latest, or else Joe would be mad at me!

All morning I was either serving people, closely overseen by Joe, running back and forth to the stockroom to replenish stock or carrying cases or whatever the customers had bought, to the bus stop or train station nearby. The weather was an important factor, as you can imagine and doing all of this on rainy days, was another thing entirely from working on nice sunny days. I can also remember some horrible winters in the late 1940's and our street, with its' pronounced downward slope was like a skating or ski run. At least once during the morning and sometimes twice (depending on Joe's mood and the sales, you understand) I would go off to the café for mugs of tea and smoked salmon beigels (note the spelling) to keep body and soul together. So, by about 1.00 to 1.30pm things would start to wind down and I could start the 'stalling in' process. This would take me until about 2.30pm trailing to and fro', carrying those cabin trunks, bags and cases, until all were packed away. At this point I was paid for the day, free to go for my late Sunday dinner, which Mum always kept hot on top of a saucepan of hot water, on the gas cooker. In my pocket was a ten-shilling note, my wages, just 50p in today's currency and of which my father allowed me to keep just two shillings, 10p and the rest went to Mum to form part of her housekeeping money for the week.

What a difference to today's culture. Can you imagine the response from the current generation of youngsters to such a regime? I doubt if many would do so much work for such small recompense, in the first place and as for giving 80% of it up, phewww! The circumstances were so, so different though, because my parents, especially my father, did not see this as their son earning a little pocket money - for himself! This was family income, without a second thought and in fact woe betide me if I even suggested otherwise!

Of course, what I did keep to myself, was the odd sixpence (2½p) or shilling tip (5p) that I earned by carrying the goods to the bus stop or railway station because there was no point in losing that by declaring it, was there? Even such paltry extras were not easily acquired, either, as I well remember on one occasion. My generous boss, Joe Goldberg, eagerly volunteered my services to deliver a cabin trunk to someone's home, in the afternoon after I had had my Sunday lunch. The fact that this customer lived in Cockfosters (North London) was no problem, because the lad (that's me!) would have no trouble finding his way and the practicalities of hauling a large cabin trunk, down onto the underground; changing trains and manhandling, (make that "boyhandling", I was all of 13/14 years old) this great trunk on and off trains, along tunnels, upstairs to ground level and along the streets to find the customer's house, seemed not to have come into old Joe's reckoning at all.

According to him, he did it to enable me to earn some extra money. So, let's just examine those two criteria, 'earn' and 'extra money'? To begin with, the round trip to Cockfosters, on the northern outskirts of London and back took me all of Sunday afternoon, utterly knackered me and as the customer had taken the trunk off me at his front door, he had thanked me and pressed a gratuity coin into my hand, which out of inbred courtesy I thanked him for but did not peruse until well clear of the house. It was a big round, shiny, silver florin and that equates to two shillings or 10p, in today's currency that glinted in my still quivering hand from the exertion of lugging that cabin trunk! "Thank you, Mr. Joe Goldberg, sir!" As a matter of fact, I was quite chuffed, really, because my expectancy levels in my boyhood days were poles apart from the demands and rights that are bandied about and expected in modern times and even the simple pleasure of a free train ride, almost into the country and back, for me, was something not to be sneezed at but part of the afternoon's reward! Do you see what I mean about expectancy and I'll bet that my contentment level was a darn sight different, as well?

MORE LIFESTYLE CHANGES

Inevitably, you will understand, some of my memories that I have committed to paper thus far overlap into several of my subtitles. As an example, some of the events or happenings I have described, are related to illustrate the changes that took place after my father returned from the war, as opposed to what was the norm before he came home but are not necessarily in the correct chronological order. Another example is my descriptions devoted to the street that we lived on, which obviously portray a period, rather than a moment in time. I have now probably filled in enough mental picture canvas, in my explanations of area, geography, atmosphere and conditions and as I go on to elucidate more upon lifestyle and activities, I will attempt to do so more in line with my growing up process and the real sequence of time. Hopefully, as and when I refer to specific places, the reader will be able to identify with the mental picture canvas, as I have termed it, as well as being able to retain a sense of the atmosphere of the times.

To emphasise my point further, I note just a brief overview concerning the activities of Sundays, as I alluded to under the subtitle of the paragraphs immediately preceding the current reading. My family, for generations on my mother's side, were practising Christians known as Plymouth Brethren and thus had strong views on the observance of Sunday as the Lord's Day. However, as is very often the case with strongly held views, of any persuasion, the practice of or compliance with those views was to varying degrees by each individual. My parents, therefore, for their own reasons allowed me to work on Sunday mornings, instead of going to Sunday morning worship and did not attend the meetings themselves, at this time either. I have no intention of being judgemental of my parents about this but, suffice to say for now that after my hard labour on Sunday mornings and the eating of my dinner, most Sundays I took my sister and myself, by bus to the Meeting Hall that we attended, for the Sunday School. As time progressed, my own convictions and beliefs prompted me to act differently and voluntarily, concerning attending a place of worship but the relating of such activity will come later, in truer chronological sequence.

So, now I will record more detail about the everyday life of the Chambers household in general and not just my own. Remember that I am at this stage dealing with the time of my first attending Grammar School, when I was around 12 to 13 years of age. Well now, all of my earlier recounting about household chores, including cleaning the home, sweeping, dusting, floor cleaning, washing up, taking the bagwash to the laundry, doing the ironing using two flat irons, heated on the gas ring of the cooker and running the errands, carried on for me right up until the time that I first went out to work – full time work, that is. I will not need to comment further on this aspect of my routines, except to say that as my nearest sister, Lillian got older, she began to share in some of these tasks and this was always necessary and expected of both of us, because my mother was never out of work herself and could never have managed to cope without our help. Most of the time, as I remember, she had 2 or even 3 different work places and it was vital that she did, because many were the weeks when it was her income alone that sustained the family, as a result of my father's gambling problems.

My younger sister, Ruth, arrived when I was just turned 11 and, as I mentioned before, many of the duties resulting from her dropping into our lives, landed upon me when Mum returned to work. To begin with I soon became an expert at preparing her feeds, made with National Dried Milk from Boots the Chemist's in Aldgate – another errand for me to run! She also had concentrated orange juice (the same as I had drunk pints of during the war as a child myself) both acquired with the aid of government issued coupons and I can still picture those milk tins and the juice bottles very clearly in my mind's eye. Nappy-changing I quickly mastered, too, as I wickedly remind her of in our mature years of the present day and, of course they were the Terry Towelling variety that had to be hand washed and boiled white but only after successfully disposing of the solid variety of waste matter – pooh! However, my lingering memory of the most exasperating job of all was when dressing her and doing up all those confounded rubber buttons on her, what was called, liberty bodice! Why they were rubber buttons, I have never been made aware, but my view is that this saved them from being cracked or crushed, when squeezed through the ringer – so popular at the time before spin and tumble driers.

Whilst on this subject of my usefulness in the home, I will reiterate what I have outlined before, which is that I can only remember being pleased to do what I was taught, then expected and needed to do, because it helped my mother and it left me with no scars of regret or abuse or discontent, as could have been the case. I am under no illusion that at times I probably felt aggrieved or even put upon and moaned a bit, too but that's not what remains in lasting memory. Some things that I did came about naturally, as well, like darning my own socks, sewing on my own buttons and simple needle repairs. This probably all stemmed from my Aunt Lily's training whilst I was at Upminster. If you recall from my earlier stories, I was encouraged and shown how to do things with needles and thread and wool etc and it all stood me in good stead. Anyway, all such activity came in handy, in later life and many that know me well nowadays, with reference to household duties and suchlike and especially my lovely wife, Jenny, will easily recognise my often-voiced claim that "my good old Mum, Nan and Aunt Lily taught me well!"

We all experience changes in lifestyle or happenings, caused by forces beyond our control and before I leave the subject of my usefulness and contribution in our home, I'll relate how the weather made life so much more difficult for us, and me in particular, in terms of heating and the water supply to our flat. I am, of course, referring to bad weather and I clearly remember several very harsh winters in the middle to late 1940's. Central heating was an unheard-of luxury in the environment of my childhood and for many years afterwards, I might add! We had small grate open fireplaces in each room and in those bitterly cold times, just guess who had the daily chore of cleaning out the ashes, relaying and lighting the fires most days? My mother left for her first cleaning job of the day before 5.00am and my father was also gone by 7.00am, which left me to do the necessary, with two younger sisters to keep warm. Incidentally, I did not envy one little bit, the job of our poor coalman who had to carry up all our stairs, the 56lb (½ cwt) sacks of coal to empty into our coal bunker on our outside rear landing and I have described elsewhere, just how many flights of stairs we had to climb. However, the poor coalman's lot was to be rivalled by me, with my father but in relation to our water supply.

The freezing weather often resulted in frozen pipes and there was no alternative, with our primitive plumbing but to collect water in buckets from the street standpipe and carry it up our stairs. My father and I, of course, did the carrying but on this occasion, he had decided that our galvanised bath full of water would, in one trip, outdo several trips carrying buckets. As you can imagine the task was very much different climbing the stairs, with him holding the handle of one end of the bath and me holding the handle at the other end of it. We made it after much puffing and blowing and all was well, until the next morning, when I could not get out of bed with a badly strained back! I seem to remember being virtually immobile for about a week – thanks Dad! With that episode related I shall leave the subject of my many and varied tasks and errands for now, at least?

SOCIAL LIFESTYLE AND ACTIVITIES

Hopefully, I have provided the reader with a taste of the sort of life that I had as a growing lad, with an emphasis leaning towards what I had to do, in terms of my contribution to the family way of life, with the occasional foray into how the intuitive young mind can turn even chores or hardship into a game or fun, to make life enjoyable. After all to put things into context, I was the eldest; I was a big strong boy, I had two younger sisters with one much younger, the post war times that we lived in were very hard times, still with rationing, living conditions in a small flat were tough, my mother was coping with up to 3 jobs every day and I had a father in full time employment but with the distorting malaise of believing that gambling would bring a better existence. On top of all this, though, I had a deep love for my mother, would do anything for her plus the extra that she hadn't asked for and an upbringing that, even at such an early time in my life, was expressing itself by an affinity with people and a desire to help and to be known and liked for it.

However, let me now turn towards describing more about my or our social lifestyle and the activities that we got up to. What did we do with our leisure time, what did I find interesting, even exciting, as I grew up towards being a young man? I shall continue to try to keep to a path that is more chronologically correct, as I go. Before we leave the recent subject of the weather, though but in relation to my new sub title I can record, that us kids also made good use of the fun aspect of weather, the snow especially. You see, apart from tobogganing on whatever slope that we could find, there was snow balling and our derivative of it, which we called 'snow bombing'.

If I tell you that our buildings had quite spacious flat roofs, if I explain that they were easily accessible by way of an iron staircase to a doorway that opened out onto the roof and if you can imagine what a large supply of crisp clean snow would collect on those flat roofs, could you begin to visualise just what snow bombing might be? I thought you might! Now there was an art to this form of mischief, which was designed to eliminate or severely reduce the risk of being caught at this dastardly exercise. You see if you were the unlucky person in the street below on the receiving end of a cold and startling snowball on the head, down your neck or whatever, you would immediately look around for the perpetrator, would you not? Not seeing one, you would probably look up but straight up in all honesty and that is just what we were banking on when we launched our snow bombs, by making sure that we threw them as far away as we could, left or right, from the spot on the roof where we were and not straight down. With an expertly launched snow bomb on its' way we just peeked over the top to view the results of our aim and with so many people milling around in the market, we rarely had a miss! The fact that our flats extended right down to the corner of our street, too, enabled us to target different sections of dense thoroughfare from the 4 streets meeting at the junction. Oh yes, we had the technique, the tactics and the escape route, all worked out if we were spotted and had loads of fun. The escape route? Why straight down one flight of stairs and into our flat, of course!

My relating the exploits of snowball bombing provides me with an opportunity to tell of more mischief, amongst the more legitimate activities, that I and we got up to. People were not the only targets to our 'bombing' pranks, because cats provided much fun and enjoyment, too! Some words of explanation are called for here, first. Another duty that fell to the responsibility of yours truly was babysitting my sisters, whenever my parents were out together – I did earlier say maybe, about writing more about my chores, didn't I? You see, probably for good marital relationship reasons my father took to taking my mother out every Saturday evening and, sometimes, another evening in the week, too. Mind you, candlelit dinners, the theatre or the cinema were never on the agenda because a budget for such niceties was never available. Dad took Mum to the 'dogs' as we called it or to put it into nicer parlance, they went greyhound racing! Such were the times when I was called upon to be in charge at home and so back to the subject of the cats.

To the rear of our flats was a yard in which were situated a long row of lock up sheds, often used by the market stallholders to store their goods in. Our back balcony looked straight down onto this yard and, remember, we were on the top floor. Some of the lock-ups had food stored in them, fruit and vegetables or packaged goods like biscuit, cakes, tinned food and pet foods, a whole variety of stuff, in fact. Understandably, rats and mice were always present, too and that's where the cats came into their own and there was no shortage of them roaming the yard. Shall we say that those members of the cat fraternity that were foolish enough to walk or wander in the area immediately below our rear balcony, were in danger of a range of unpleasant surprises! The landing on them of the contents of a small bowl of water was sure to splash, startle and soak, for example. Whereas, the landing of small lumps of coal that 'exploded' alongside or near to a slumbering cat, had startling results. That was cruel, you might say but we did it as harmless fun and never aimed to directly hit the poor animals, did we?!

I remember variations, too, of this mischief, which was to startle people walking through the courtyard of the flats that backed onto our buildings but the ammunition for this was usually small round potatoes! On one occasion my aim was off target but still particularly good, as the missile that I launched went straight through the open kitchen window of the ground floor flat opposite, landing with a big 'plop' in this lady's bowl of washing up water, as she stood at the sink. I dodged out of sight before she looked up and saw me, so I missed viewing the likely resulting splash, but it must have been spectacular! Thankfully, we never got spotted or caught and how we managed that, as I think about it now, I will never know – just being crafty EastEnders, perhaps? Especially, as I sometimes used to leave my sisters in the flat and go down to the same courtyard and play football with the boys, watched by my sisters from our balcony, so that I could keep an eye on them.

Of course, some of these mischievous activities were carried out when Mum and Dad were out 'socialising', that is when Dad took Mum with him to greyhound racing and such mischief would not have been allowed with Mum at home! Speaking of 'socialising' reminds me that from time to time we would exchange visits with our relations who lived in the flats almost diagonally opposite across our street. They were my mother's brother, wife and 2 daughters – Uncle Les, Auntie Marie and cousins Carol and Beverley. We would have an evening meal together and then the adults would play cards (a game called Solo) or the men played darts, while the women chatted. The girls, my 2 sisters and 2 cousins did girlie things whilst I joined in with the darts matches, being almost then and later a real teenager! Things changed with the advent of TV, although it had less effect on the men who continued with their darts matches. Also, when it was our turn to entertain in our flat, apart from the change that TV brought, the arrival of the ¼ size billiard/snooker table that Dad purchased on HP, also meant this taking over as far as the men were concerned. Mind you, even in our largish 'front room', negotiating the table, especially at each corner, with the cue end often almost disappearing into a sitting person's ear, eye or nose made for some strange happenings to add to the fun! One last memory regarding the two families' ability to communicate quickly and before the arrival of 'the phone'. If or whenever my mother or aunt wanted each other, either would throw up their front room window and in a strident, clarion-call kind of shout, screech out the name, "*Gertieeeeeeeee*" or "*Marieeeeeeee*" and the whole of Petticoat Lane, including passers-by, would be party to the ensuing conversation, between two ladies, conducted some 60 odd feet up at the top of the buildings - Oh, such happy days!

For a long period of time, several years in fact, during the growing up period of my life and the lives of my two sisters and after the return to becoming a family unit following my father's war service, I was an important part of the family's day to day running. As I have explained elsewhere, my mother was occupied with holding down 3 jobs, usually coming home from her last one at around 9 to 9.30pm; my father left for work early morning, had something like an hour's journey to work across in West London and rarely came home before late evening (usually between 10 & 11 pm). This was partly due to working overtime but mostly due to his weekday evening visits to greyhound racing. Therefore, my evenings were almost exclusively spent babysitting and for my younger sister that was from a baby age – feeding, bathing, nappy changing, the lot! Some of the things that I and we got up to I have recounted but they mostly relate to summer or the lighter evenings. The long dark winter evenings were another matter altogether and many long hours had to be whiled away, either us kids on our own or when either or both of our parents were at home.

Too much detail of this would be a bore so I will just highlight some activities that occupied us, leaving the reader to determine which would have been indulged in whilst with parental presence or as otherwise. One of the issues that I have with present day situations is the absolute glut that there is of anything and everything that one could ever want – especially children. This is not the cue for a huge, melodramatic wail of "Poor you". However, it does illustrate my point when I tell you that between them, I doubt if my two sisters had more than 2 or 3 dolls to play with and I only ever remember 1 small doll's pram and maybe a couple of changes of clothes to dress the dolls and swap with. As for me, I had a prize collection of 3 Dinky toys – a Scammell flatbed truck, a Ford Popular car and my pride and joy, a 'mechanical horse', in British Rail livery. The last named, for the uninformed being a 3-wheeler tractor unit, pulling a canvas covered trailer

– still in use today. These three items, several boxes of matches and oodles of imagination kept me occupied for hours on end.

The matches placed end to end formed a kitchen table full of road network over which to run my small transport fleet. A small square of cardboard, about 3" by 3" with cotton from all 4 corners connected to a single strand, formed my lift to raise and lower a vehicle between table top and the floor and so extend the road network. Sometimes, we would need to "let off steam", so it would be an obstacle course around that snooker table that I told you of earlier, just chasing each other over chairs and stepping on cushions etc. Another great pastime was standing at the head of Mum and Dad's big double bed and just crashing face down and counting the number of times that you bounced after landing and which lead to an amusing but fateful happening on one such an occasion! As I crash-landed full stretch on the bed, it jerked away from against the wall and one of the legs cracked halfway up its' length! You can imagine the anguish and consternation which followed, and I had to set to work with string and tape to bind the wooden leg at the break. Fortunately, with the broken leg being at the head of the bed, it was against the wall and easier to hide from sight. I, of course, told my mother about it and she colluded to keep the offence hidden from Dad, unbelievably, for many weeks before he discovered it! I cannot recall what happened when he did find out, or perhaps I prefer to blot it out? Which leads me to conclude this recourse into questionable activity whilst I was 'in charge'.

As I and my sisters got older, so my custodial responsibilities for them got a little less or more varied and interesting. In the light evenings the girls could play in the street and the play areas behind the flats, under the watchful eye of my mother – no prizes for guessing where my father was most evenings? So, I could roam more with my mates and we would go off all over the City area on our home-made ball-bearing wheeled scooters. Great fun on the smooth asphalt pavements and the empty streets with all the offices closed for the day. As I've mentioned before, bombed out buildings were also a paradise for us to explore and make camps in and dodging the 'cops' was a great part of that fun – we were the virtually 'uncatchable!' As far as the dark or winter evenings are concerned, I have already related something of what we got up to, except for when the girls were growing up more and with me being allowed to take them off to the 'pictures'. This was mostly on Saturday evenings and, although we went to several local cinemas, by far the most frequented was 'The Popular' cinema, as it was grandly called, in Stepney along Commercial Road – the proverbial 'Flea Pit!' The reason for that – price! I could take both sisters and me by bus, there and back; pay the entrance price and buy a bag of chips each to eat on the bus home, for a grand sum of less than 5/- or 25p! By the way, we saw an 'A' film; a 'B' film, a documentary, a cartoon and extensive 'Forthcoming Attractions', as they were called. Plus, if you got in early enough, when the programme was finished you got out of your seat, went to the toilet, came back and sat somewhere else (to bamboozle the usherette) and watched the whole thing all over again, for the same entrance price!

Another outlet for me, as a growing lad, came in the form of an unexpected knock on the door one day, by the Curate of the local church, Christchurch, Spitalfields. His name was Fred Nevelle and he was on the look-out for candidates to attend a new club that he was opening at the Church. Essentially, in his case, for boys although one already existed for similar aged girls, the two were part of a national Christian organisation called 'Covenanters' prefixed by Boy or Girl, of course. These were the seniors aged 12 to 18 and the juniors were also catered for from 8 to 12 as Junior Covenanters or 'Jucos'. As well as a Sunday afternoon meeting or Bible Class the organisation had an extensive range of club type activities to cater for energetic kids and teenagers to join in with and be part of.

There were rallies, summer and winter 'camps', many sports to partake in, organised outings and weekly club activities to go to and enjoy. On a few occasions, such as weekly Club evenings, the boys and girls' clubs would meet together for table tennis, billiards, snooker, board games etc with refreshments and chatter thrown in. As you can imagine such an opportunity was grabbed by me with two strong and willing hands! Many a great time was had, for the next few years, when I was able to join up to play football matches, go camping, learn to play table tennis etc and expend tons of youthful energy in a safe and moral environment. I suppose, though, that the most significant single outcome of joining the Covenanters was to come when I reached the age of 16½ years of age. One club evening, whilst playing a game of table tennis with a friend, Roger, a fellow Covenanter, he introduced me to his girlfriend, Joan. She, in turn, when the game had finished, introduced me to her friend, Eileen. I am sure that, by now as you read, you will connect with what comes next! Yes, Eileen became my girlfriend and 5 years later, after I came out of the RAF, my first wife. So, the 4 of us, all Covenanters, began a foursome that lasted through until the two marriages sent us on our separate ways, as so often happens. But that is jumping the gun!

Another 'escape' for me, from household chores, was to be able to go to my Aunt Lily and Uncle Bert's at Upminster, straight from school every Wednesday evening. This was the evening when the former members of the Sunday School and older Bible Class of the church attended by my Aunt and Uncle, carried on their weekly social meeting and which I, of course, was always present at when I lived there during the war years. They were all about 3 years older than me, but I was no longer the nipper of the wartime days but almost a teenager myself and the age gap was less significant. We always had a fun time and I would stay the night and go straight to school, back to London, the next morning.

At this stage in my writings, I must put on record how a lifelong passion began for me and one that was part of my family, too, long before I first took breath. I became another follower of that incomparable football team – 'the' Arsenal! As any older generation of hardened football fan will tell you, Arsenal were the 'glamour boys' of London and the envy of all

North of Watford! After all, they had those two imposing stands, 'modern' dressing rooms with proper baths and showers and from back in the 1930's that was, when other well-known and famous teams were far less well equipped. In those heady days of my first allegiance, recruited by my father and my Uncle Les, in time for the 1946 season, it was to the 'Gunners', in modern times adapted to the 'Gooners' that I went to watch in becoming a football fan.

I went to Highbury, the Gunners' home, every Saturday without missing, to all 'home' games whenever played and that regularity only faltered when full time employment intervened or National Service, of course. I alternated between watching the first team playing at home one week and the 'reserves' playing the next week. We always stood at the tube station end of the ground, long before the days when it was covered and became known as the 'North Bank'. I will always remember the excitement that I felt as we, or I, travelled from Aldgate East District line Underground station, to Kings Cross and changed there onto the Piccadilly Tube line to Arsenal station, the only football club on the planet to have an underground station named after it! Joining the crowds spilling out of the train, walking up the long passenger tunnel to street level, through the ticket barrier and into Gillespie Road. It was always madly busy with throngs of fans but much more so on the days when the first team were in town. Without exception, on those days, the queue to get into the North end of the ground went all the way along Gillespie Road to turn right up Avenell Road and almost to outside the main entrance to the Stadium – about 250 yards.

Then there were the queues, once inside the outer gates, to get through the turnstiles. I cannot remember precisely but I think it was about one shilling for me, under 16, to get into the stadium – that's 5 new pence and on the 'reserve team' days it was even less. Many a time after going through the turnstiles, when we had climbed the stairs to the top of the terrace, the crowd was so thickly packed that it was difficult for a young lad to see the pitch. So, youngsters like me were passed over the heads of fans until reaching the front, down by the railings and right behind the goal.

From there I would look up at those two fantastic stands and my lasting memory is of thinking to myself that I would never, ever be able to afford to sit in a seat in those stands, not ever! The passing of time changes things, however and many years later I was to become the holder of two season tickets, in the East stand, in the front row, right where the TV cameras were stationed and often chatted with the likes of the TV commentator, Brian Moore.

To carry on, so near to the pitch just behind the goal, I would be really close to many players, now legends of old but the idols of my day. Players like Raich Carter, Stanley Matthews, Stan Mortenson, Wilf Mannion, Billy Wright, Tom Finney, Tommy Lawton etc. Then there were the 'greats' of the Arsenal team, as well and the whole team that I remember from that time would have looked like this: George Swindon in goal; Laurie Scott and Bernard Joy as full backs, Leslie Compton: centre half, Joe Mercer and Alec Forbes the half backs, Denis Compton and Ian McPherson as wingers, Bryn Jones and Jimmy Logie the inside forwards and Reg Lewis centre forward. I also remember seeing Cliff Bastin, George Male, Kevin O'Flanagan (Dr.), Ronnie Rooke, Don Roper and Archie Macaulay etc, etc. My allegiance to Arsenal has never changed or even wavered to this day. It is a matter of history that we finished 13th out of the 21 teams in the First Division of that time, in that year of 1946/7. I remain a 'Gooner' to this day, even though the difficulty in getting to their home ground, now the Emirates Stadium, from Folkestone where I now live is the reason for my much-reduced level of personal attendance, but there is always the TV, enabling me to view many matches.

Inevitably, I seem to be nearing the end of my attempt to try and paint the picture of my early life and am now approaching the full adolescent stage. I had entered this world at a point in time that resulted in a very varied, somewhat fraught and often dangerous childhood. As with many like me, the needs of the times and family circumstances precluded any thoughts of higher education to include college or university. I was taken out of grammar school at 16½ years of age, with just 4 GCE 'O' levels to my name (English Language, French, German and Geography) and firmly encouraged into work, beginning as a junior Bank Clerk with Lloyds Bank.

After just 2 months at my first branch, in Upper Street, Islington, I was packed off to the Lloyds Bank Training Centre in Hindhead, Surrey. Perched right on the perimeter edge of the beauty spot there, the Devil's Punchbowl, it was like having a posh holiday for a duration of 8 weeks! The biggest benefit by far, though, was playing football and basketball for the Centre in the local leagues. I passed out from there as a fully trained Bank Clerk, including the qualification of being proficient in the latest NCR and Burrough's accounting machines – the forerunners of computerisation. But... and this is a big 'but!' I was then posted to a tiny, scruffy branch in Stoke Newington, North London, boasting only a weather-beaten old Bank Manager, a miserable Chief Clerk, 1 male and 2 lady Cashiers and, to cap it all, entirely handwritten! The only 'apology' for being at all mechanical was several hand operated adding machines! It had central heating, mind you, if you can count lighting and stoking the boiler fire, all day in the cellar as such? My Job Description, if there had been one, would have amounted to 4 daily tasks, as follows:

1) Light and keep stoked, the boiler in the cellar.
2) Answer the branch telephone.
3) Make the tea at prescribed and required times.
4) Complete and maintain the 'Daily Waste Sheet'

Three of these tasks are self-explanatory, but the fourth needs serious explanation! The day's business of any bank must balance, come what may – no if's or but's, it must balance. Every single transaction, be it cash, cheques, bonds, drafts, whatever in or out of the branch that day must balance, and nobody goes home until it does – to the penny!

The huge sheet of paper that recorded every single movement, of whatever, through the branch that day was called the Daily Waste Sheet. Some 24 inches wide by about 12 inches from top to bottom, it had umpteen columns, and all needed to be added up and balanced across the whole sheet, at the close of business, on the stroke of 3 o'clock. Of course, any normal day's business would result in a good number of these sheets, with all the totals carried forward onto new sheets to arrive at the final figures for the day on the last sheet. Can you imagine just what was involved when the final balancing act was carried out and the resultant furore if, as was often the case, the darned thing DID NOT BALANCE!

Have you any idea, too, what it felt like every day, with the entire branch staff, waiting for Junior Bank Clerk Chambers to agree and balance the Daily Waste Sheet and the pain and turmoil when it did not balance? Those stomach wrenching moments, just after 3.00 pm every day were unrivalled in dread, except by the sound of the branch manager's voice, at any time of the day calling *"Chambers – the boiler's gone out!"* Is it really any wonder that my tenure as a fully trained Bank Clerk and competent Accounting Machine Operator, no less, with Lloyds Bank Ltd lasted just 9 months before I packed it in? Maybe part of me, though, just did not take very kindly to being just a 'dogsbody' after all, to be quite honest?

So, now what? Just 9 months or so to go before my 18th. birthday required me to be prepared for call-up into the armed forces to do my National Service. Well, for certain, I had to get another job as, in my world, there was no such thing as 'living off' the parents for those few months. So, I got another job with the Co-operative Wholesale Society (CWS) the wholesale arm of the 'Co-op' in Spitalfields Wholesale Fruit & Vegetable Market, initially as a Pricing Clerk under training to become a Wholesale Buyer. The job was to purchase produce for onward sales to the various retail Co-op societies' shops. The 3 main Societies in and around London being;

London Co-op. Society, Royal Arsenal Co-op. Society and South Suburban Co-op Society which amounted to some 500 plus outlets in total.

I thoroughly enjoyed my time with the 'Co-op' and I was to return from my 2-year stint in the RAF to resume work there for several more years. The unusual hours were much to my liking - the market operated from 05.00 am to around 02.00 pm, Monday to Friday but I was always finished around 01.00 pm and on Saturday I was always off home by 10.00 am. This suited me handsomely, on Saturdays because I had time to rest and prepare to play football for the CWS team, that competed in the London Business Houses League. I was already more than a competent player, having played for Lloyds Bank, too, during my employment with them and soon became the skipper, as a dominant centre half! The CWS had a wonderfully equipped sports ground and Social Club at Woolston Hall, Chigwell, Essex where we played all our 'home' games and trained 2 evenings a week. In the summer months it was cricket and I was a 'demon' medium/fast bowler! At both Lloyds and the CWS, I also carried on competing at the Shot-Putt and Javelin events in their respective Athletics Clubs and events.

My friendship with Eileen, who was to become my first wife, probably began to develop into something more relational by now. The foursome outings that I have mentioned previously, with respective friends, Roger and Joan were quite frequent and we saw each other often during the week and at weekend outings. She lived with her mother and older sister in the flats above the trader's warehouses around the perimeter of Spitalfields Market, but her father had died when she was only a child. By the time, therefore, that my civilian life was to be forcibly interrupted by governmental command and thrust into two years of conscription, Eileen and I were a 'couple', as they say!

Things began to physically move towards the dreaded call-up, as well, by my getting the summons to a Recruitment Centre in Woodford in early March 1953, coincident with my 18th. Birthday. There, with many others, I underwent a full medical which I passed as A1; a short education and aptitude test, which also posed no problem and a discussion to ascertain if I had any preferences for what I was to be employed at or as, for the next 2 years. On this subject, I soon was able to ascertain from others going through the proceedings ahead of me, that a personal 'choice' was largely immaterial to what was designated! So, for me it was like this. I did not fancy the Army with the prospect of 'foot slogging', firing guns and being shot at etc. The Navy was not a pleasant prospect, either, for me a person with anything but a liking for depths of water below me, despite the attraction of foreign climes to visit. The Air Force, however, was a real preference for me because of my love for and fascination with, anything aeronautical. So, what happened about all this? Well, in broad summary, as follows. I got accepted into the Royal Air Force, Fighter Command, in Fighter Control and because of a Grammar School education, I was drafted into what was termed as POM Flight and initially posted to RAF Hednesford, in Staffordshire for my 8 weeks Initial Training – more commonly known as 'Square-bashing'.

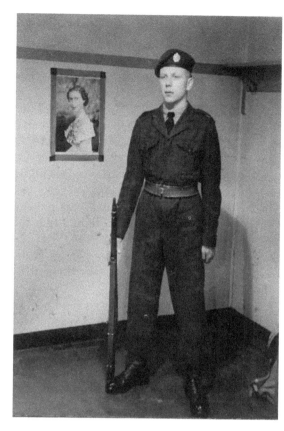

This is at RAF Hednesford in Staffs. in the 'on guard' pose, in the 'at ease' position, as it was called. Note the Queen's portrait photo on the wall – it was, of course, Coronation year.

From there I was to go on to RAF Middle Wallop, for another 4 weeks, to be trained in Fighter Control, then to the Air Firing School at RAF Acklington. When a brand-new, top-secret station, part of the NATO Radar Early Warning Chain, RAF Boulmer was opened I moved on to there, where I was promoted to CCA (Chief Controller's Assistant) Both of these stations being in the lovely county of Northumberland. Here we controlled Fighter Pilots learning their trade as interceptors of hostile aircraft, by radar, plotting and radio telecommunication or R/T, whilst also keeping a wary eye on the movements of Russian "intruders" of NATO and UK airspace. There I stayed in lovely Northumberland until the last 2 months of my service, when I was posted to RAF Uxbridge. Here I worked logging all movements of military aircraft and liaising with civilian Air Traffic Controllers at London Airport. I also got home much more frequently and most weekends especially!

By the way, you may still be querying in your mind just what POM might stand for, at my initial posting? Potential Officer Material – no less! But, for me, it was never a possibility as 'signing-on' for a minimum of 3 years' service was not in my reckoning, and my background was lacking in finesse and status to boot. To be more explicit, very few purely National Service (2 years only) personnel were granted a commission, with just 1 person per POM Flight being the norm. Secondly, the successful person from our POM Flight just happened to be the son of a regular serving officer in the RAF – a Group Captain, as well! So, what chance for anyone else, anyway?

So there, my destiny for the next 2 years was set, and I've recorded prematurely how it did pan out, over that period, as a result of that day at the Recruitment Centre in Woodford. These writings also amount to an account of my life, remembered in fairly comprehensive detail, from first recollections until just turned 20 years of age. For me, though and for many thousands of other young men of my era, National Service was an added, non-voluntary life experience that had influence and affect not always recognised or understood. If it was more universally realised and properly evaluated, in my view, it would and should still be in existence!

I truly believe that the deeper and long-term benefits, for the vast majority who served, were definite and for the better. Like everything in life, though, there are exceptions that prove the rule, as legend has it. As for me and my opinion, well, not difficult to understand really. The benefits outweighed the non-benefits, both for me as a person and as a life experience to learn from – simply that, except for the most significant benefit for me, above all else. That is the invaluable blessing of giving my life to Christ when I was only just a young boy, 8½ years old! I readily say, no, I readily shout it from the rooftops, the words of the song **"My Jesus, my Saviour, Lord, there is none like you"**

One thought and one observation about that reflective moment on Euston Station – did all this really happen in just 18 years? Plus, it's taken some 3 years or more, to research, recall, write up, edit, re-edit and then sign off! Finally, if you have read these writings right through, then you have done well. Thank you and I hope that it was worth the read!

Eddie Chambers
Cheriton, Folkestone, Kent

November 2018

Extra Insights

This is Eddie at RAF Middle Wallop, Hants, basic Training completed (otherwise known as 'square bashing') He was here for an 8-week course to become a Fighter Plotter and ultimately Chief Controller's Assistant on a Radar station, RAF Boulmer. (June 1953)

This is Eddie at RAF, Boulmer in Northumberland, in March 1955, lounging on the doorpost, some few weeks before transfer to RAF Uxbridge to be demobbed back into 'civvy street'.

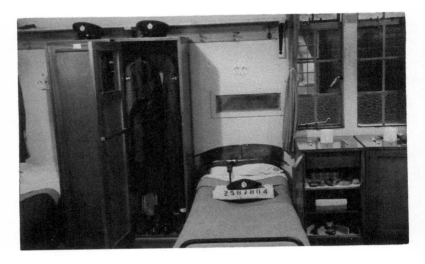

Eddie's bed-space in the billet with 30 odd other 'sprogs' – the nickname for new recruits! On the left of the picture: the wardrobe locker, the bed and the bedside locker on the right. This photo was taken just before what was known as a 'billet inspection', hence the precise layout of all kit and personal property, in place. The even more dreaded 'kit inspection' involved the precise layout of everything on the bed, leaving the 2 lockers empty for a closer look!

Finally,

A short poem I came across of an unknown author, but I think it bears particular impact in the context of this story, a light-hearted summation of "the old days" ...

I REMEMBER...

I remember corned beef in
 my childhood;
And the bread that we cut
 with a knife,
When children helped out
 with the housework,
And the men went to
 work, not the wife!
When the cheese never
 needed a fridge;
And the bread was so
 crusty and hot,
When children were
 seldom unhappy,
Wife and mother was
 content with her lot.

I remember the milk from
 a bottle;
With thick yummy cream
 on the top,
Our dinner came hot from
 the oven,
And not from the freezer
 or a shop.
Us kids were a lot more
 contented;

They didn't need money
 for kicks,
Just games with their
 friends in the roadway,
And maybe, on Saturday,
 the flicks?

I remember the slaps on
 my backside;
And the taste of the soap if
 I dared swear!
Anorexia and diets weren't
 even heard of,
And rarely a choice what
 to wear!
Do you think this all
 bruised our ego?
Maybe initiative
 destroyed?
When you ate what was
 put on the table,
I think life then was better
 enjoyed.

Unknown Author

Lightning Source UK Ltd.
Milton Keynes UK
UKHW010646300619
345236UK00002BA/112/P